SENIOR YEAR

Books by Anne Emery

Sally & Jean Burnaby Series
Senior Year
Going Steady
Sorority Girl
High Note Low Note
Campus Melody

Jane Ellison Series
County Fair
Hickory Hill
Sweet Sixteen

Pat Marlowe Series
First Love True Love
First Orchid for Pat
First Love Farewell

Dinny Gordon Series
Dinny Gordon, Freshman
Dinny Gordon, Sophomore
Dinny Gordon, Junior
Dinny Gordon, Senior

Sue Morgan Books
The Popular Crowd
The Losing Game

Non-Series Books
Scarlet Royal
Vagabond Summer
That Archer Girl

Married on Wednesday
A Dream to Touch

Tradition
Bright Horizons
Mountain Laurel

Jennie Lee, Patriot

American Friend: Herbert Hoover

Mystery of the Opal Ring
Danger in a Smiling Mask
Carey's Fortune
The Sky Is Falling
Free Not to Love
Stepfamily

Spy Series
A Spy in Old Philadelphia
A Spy in Old Detroit
A Spy in Old New Orleans
A Spy in Old West Point

SENIOR YEAR

by ANNE EMERY

Illustrated by Beth Krush

Image Cascade Publishing

www.ImageCascade.com

MANUFACTURED IN THE UNITED STATES
OF AMERICA

A hardcover edition of this book was originally
published by The Westminster Press. It is here
reprinted by arrangement with Joan Emery Sanders.

First *Image Cascade Publishing* edition published 2005.

Library of Congress Cataloging in Publication Data
Emery, Anne 1907–1987
     Senior year.

(Juvenile Girls)
Reprint. Originally published: Philadelphia:
Westminster Press, 1949.

ISBN 978-1-59511-005-3 (Pbk.)

SENIOR YEAR

SALLY BURNABY raced up the stairs and dropped two suitcases inside her room. She drew a deep breath and exhilaration bubbled up inside of her like soda water. This was the most wonderful part of the whole vacation: getting home again! And she couldn't wait another minute to talk to Kate Kennicott and find out all the news.

Pulling the upstairs telephone inside her room, she sprawled on her bed, with the phone on her chest, and dialed. Plans for the coming weeks flashed across her mind: shopping with Kate for a new reversible; getting together with the gang — maybe there'd be time for one more swim and beach picnic before the weather changed; double dating at the first dance of the year with Kate and Ted; the opening football game.

The line was busy.

With an exasperated sigh, she put the telephone on the bedside table and sat up. Outside her window she could hear six-year-old Jimmy clamoring for his bicycle. Right away!

"Relax, sonny," she heard her father advise him unsympathetically. "These bags have to get into the house first, and someone will have to find the garage key."

Sally went to her window and looked down at Juniper Lane. The lawns were wide and green, under the overhanging elms. It was a golden September day, perfect for home-coming. In the mellow sunlight the trees glowed with the first bright hint of changing color.

In front of the house the rest of the Burnabys were busy around the travel-worn green Ford sedan. Dad looked genial and quite informal in the sport shirt and tan slacks he had worn for driving. Sally grinned as she watched him, slender and wiry, swinging the bags out of the trunk with the gay energy of home-coming. Sometimes you'd never think he was a dignified college professor.

Mother, looking like one of the girls, with her trim figure and dark hair, was inspecting the lawn. She claimed it was impossible to grow a decent lawn with all those trees, but she kept trying every year.

Nine-year-old Betsy, swinging long black braids, was struggling with two heavy bags.

"They're too heavy," called dad, when he saw her. "Leave them for Rick. Where is he?"

He was nowhere in sight. Somewhere downstairs, Sally could hear him rummaging through drawers for the garage key to get out his own bicycle.

She turned from the window. Home, sweet home! The sentiment might be corny, but it was certainly true. She especially loved her room, which she shared with Jean.

For her birthday present last spring, mother had redecorated the room. She had made a skirt for the vanity and spreads for the twin beds, letting Sally choose the color scheme and pick out material. Jean didn't care, so Kate had helped Sally find the white chintz with red poppies. Later the three of them had painted the dresser and desk and also a chair to match the red of the poppies. Kate had loved the green-and-white striped paper and the red corduroy lounge chair. Painting the inside of the white bookcase the dull green of the wallpaper had been her suggestion.

That's how it was: ever since they had gone to grade

school together Kate had helped Sally choose clothes and wallpaper and slip covers and books and friends.

Anticipating how the room would look when Jean's things were spread around, Sally winced. Why did her sister have to be so completely opposite? She had been working on Jean for years now, but the results were scarcely perceptible. With a small frown of regret, Sally picked up the telephone again. Someone was already talking. Jean, of course, on the downstairs phone. Sally cradled the instrument in annoyance. No telling now when she'd get another chance! She might as well unpack.

Opening the big bag on the floor, she meticulously sorted things out: these for the house laundry; those for the bathroom laundry; brush and comb, powder, and cream for the dressing-table drawer. With a piece of kleenex, Sally carefully dusted off the glass top, reminiscing over the pictures under the glass as she bent over it: small picture strips of Kate and of Scotty, snaps of the crowd at the beach party a year ago, the eighth-grade graduating class three years back (didn't we look like children?), the church choir in gowns and caps.

It would be fun to see Scotty again, even though she had hardly thought of him during the summer. She studied a strip of five small pictures, showing his head in different positions. He wasn't handsome, certainly, but there was something very attractive about his red hair and wide grin and independent manner. He was just the boy who lived down the street, but they had always had fun together.

Someone was bumping up the stairs. So Jean was through with the telephone! Sally reached for it at once, and put it down again. Better go downstairs after all, where she could be alone. She'd just finish picking up first.

Her sister pushed open the door and stumbled in, dragging her bag heavily over the threshold. Jean's hair drooped over her eyes, her hands were grubby, and she dropped her bag with a groan and collapsed into the red easy chair.

"Jean!" Sally had made firm resolutions every night of their trip not to nag at Jean any more. But this time she couldn't help herself. "Your jeans are filthy. You look simply awful! Aren't you going to clean up and unpack?"

"Who cares?" yawned Jean, her feet, in thick socks and dirty saddle shoes, sprawling over most of the floor.

"Oh, honestly!" Sally snapped. "I don't see how you can stand it! All you have to do is to clean up a little!"

"Go fly a kite!" Jean instructed her in lazy cheerfulness. "I'm tired, and I want to lie down and read a good book!"

Sally turned impatiently to the dressing table and sat down to brush her black hair again. She studied her reflection with some satisfaction: Her face was a little rounder than she liked, but her skin was clear and glowing; her color was just right; her eyebrows had character, the girls told her; and her hair was very satisfactory: glossy and softly waving to her shoulders, caught back from a middle part with small flowered barrettes; brown eyes; good teeth, thanks to those braces she used to complain about so bitterly; a nice wide mouth.

She would have been pleased if her size fourteen figure had dwindled painlessly to a twelve, but really it wasn't worth dieting about just yet: maybe next year, if she had to, before she went to college.

But Jean — Sally could see her in the mirror, slouched all over the chair, disheveled and unwashed, reading her book. Sally's considered opinion was that her sister was hopeless. It wasn't just that she never picked things up and never closed her dresser drawers entirely and never put shoe trees in her shoes; those things at least Sally could bear, in the bosom of the family. But she refused to do anything about her hair. Said she hadn't time — she'd rather read. She wouldn't put on lipstick. And she didn't care if she wore the same dress two days in a row, when everyone knew *that* simply was not done.

Complaining to mother did no good. She said unsympathetically: "You'd get much farther if you'd stop picking on your sister, Sally. I know just how she feels — you make her contrary."

The telephone rang sharply, and Sally caught it hopefully on the second ring. A voice asked for Mrs. Burnaby.

Sally found her mother in the garden looking at the results of the summer's neglect — a trowel in her hand.

"I suppose it's hopeless by this time," she said with a frown, straightening up as Sally came out of the house. "Look at these weeds! But I would like a nice fall garden. We should have flowers until frost!"

"Telephone, mother! Why don't you wait until tomorrow, when you have your gardening clothes on?"

Mother was something to rejoice in — young-looking as another sister, tolerant and easy to talk to. She seemed to know how things happened without being told. And she had as much energy as one of the high-school crowd, running a house and five children with one hand and three organizations and a garden with the other.

She laid down her trowel, rubbed her soiled hands regretfully, and went into the house. Sally followed, to wait her turn at the telephone. Home almost an hour and still she hadn't talked to Kate! Of course she could go down and see her — it was only three doors away. But Sally couldn't run out on the family the moment she got home. She'd better phone first, and get together with Kate tonight.

She went over and softly fingered the keys on the small old upright piano. Jean was the only one in the family who really knew how to play — except mother, of course. Sally wished now that she could play as well as Jean. But there never seemed to be time to practice.

Mother waved a warning hand and Sally went into the sunroom and flipped on the radio. She had never realized how pretty the living room was, she thought, twisting the dials idly. The chintz-covered Victorian chairs and the walls of bookshelves were lovely. And that oil portrait of Sally, aged seven, over the mantel.

Her mother was still talking.

"Oh, isn't that too bad! . . . Yes, I know I'm the vice-president. But I never expected — well, all right, let's have a board meeting next Tuesday. At two . . ."

"Where's Betsy?" asked Mrs. Burnaby, leaving the telephone. "I haven't seen her since she took her bag upstairs."

She called up the steps, and somewhere behind a closed door on the second floor, Sally could hear a muffled response.

"She's right here, then," Mrs. Burnaby checked her off.

"Could I talk to Kate now?" Sally asked wistfully.

Her mother laughed. "My goodness, haven't you had a chance to talk to her yet? Go ahead! But keep it short. You can see her tonight." Thankfully, Sally shut herself in the closet with the telephone and dialed Kate's number again. At last!

"Hello!" she cried, after six long rings. "Kate? We're home! . . . Oh, we had a wonderful time! I've got loads to tell you. How about tonight? . . . What's the news around here?

"What did you say? Kate! Oh, no! "

Numbly she listened to Kate's familiar voice, chattering on at the other end of the wire. It couldn't be true. It just couldn't!

"Well, yes — " she said drearily, as Kate stopped talking, "I suppose it will be fun for you. But it'll ruin every-

[13]

thing for me. Oh, it's too awful! . . . O.K., I'll be along tonight. Good-by now."

Sally replaced the telephone and sagged in her chair. Kate's unexpected news was a stunning blow. With a dazed feeling, she went to look for her mother in the kitchen.

"Mother!" she exclaimed tragically. "The most awful thing — "

Mrs. Burnaby waved a frantic hand at her, writing with the other and thinking out loud.

"Could you save it just a minute?" she begged. "It's nearly five o'clock and I've got to figure out what we'll need from the store — hamburger, potatoes, frozen limas, lettuce — "

Sally watched her in silence. It was useless to tell mother something at the wrong time. This was bad enough news for Sally to keep to herself until her audience was in a receptive mood.

"Ice cream for dessert," mother was still writing. "Oranges for breakfast, bacon, eggs, bread, butter — are you sure you can manage all this on your bike?"

"I can manage," said Sally, taking the list.

She wheeled her bike out of the garage, around the welter of doll buggies, scooters, a tangled tennis net, two basketballs, and some loose croquet balls and wickets, and rode out on Juniper Lane.

Jimmy was riding his small two-wheeled sidewalk bike erratically up and down. He had already collected his six-year-old crony from the end of the block, who was watching him critically, waiting for his turn on the bike. Kate was nowhere in sight, nor was Scotty, and Sally pedaled briskly off, thinking somberly about the bad news she had not yet had a chance to tell. Naturally mother wouldn't think it was so bad. Grownups were like that — they didn't understand the really important things like friends and dates and clothes. When she reached the store, Sally forgot her worries for a while. It was fun to greet the clerks again, who knew all the Burnabys, and to feel welcomed home.

As she rode back with the groceries stacked carefully in her basket, a gang of small boys playing baseball in the park made her think of Rick, who had not been seen since they arrived. She hoped he would turn up in time for dinner. He seldom did, and it was becoming a critical issue when they had left on their trip, in June.

When she came in to dump the groceries, she found Jean setting the table.

"I'll fix the centerpiece," Sally offered. She loved arranging flowers. In the garden she chose white and yellow chrysanthemums, and achieved an arrangement in a low yellow bowl before Jean finished the table. Then she discovered that Jean had used pink place mats, and refused to change them just to carry out Sally's color scheme.

"All right, then," said Sally, with conscious patience, "only it would be nice to have the first dinner at home as perfect as possible."

"Why didn't you pick pink flowers?" asked Jean.

Sally ignored her and changed the mats herself. Then she went out into the kitchen again, where mother, looking slightly harried, was stirring the gravy. All of a sudden Sally felt depressed again with her bad news.

"Mother," she began importantly, seating herself on the step stool, "Kate told me the most awful thing today — "

"Will you take the potatoes off, dear? They're about to burn."

Mother hadn't heard a word she'd said. Sally leaped for the potatoes, grabbed a holder, and moved them, and found herself being handed the masher. Mr. Burnaby came out to the kitchen, asking vaguely if he could be helpful. There was no use trying to talk just now.

"Dad, if you'll pour the milk, please!" Mother had forgotten to dress the salad, and was mixing oil and vinegar with quick strokes.

"We're just about ready," she said hopefully. "Will you round up the children, Jean? Where's Betsy?"

Jean glanced at the clock.

"Listening to Captain Midnight."

Mrs. Burnaby sighed and went back to dishing up the food.

"I know you girls finally outgrew Superman and Captain Midnight, but sometimes I lose faith," she said pessimistically. "It seems as if Captain Midnight will be with us until Betsy has grandchildren. Really, I thought she might forget him during the months we've been away —"

"Not a chance," said Jean. "He's her favorite hero, mother, and you know Betsy is tenacious and loyal."

"Good qualities, no doubt," said her mother dryly, "I just wish she'd fasten them on somebody else. I'd rather have her reading a good book."

"Oh, she's doing that too," Jean assured her. "I always did."

Somehow they were all at the table finally, except one, while the hot food was still hot and the cold salad crisp.

"Isn't this where we came in?" asked Mr. Burnaby, looking around his family solemnly. "I think I've seen this picture before."

Sally took a long drink of milk, feeling slightly pained. She didn't think her father was nearly as cute as the girls told her he was. Some of his jokes were very flat. Betsy, pried away from her radio drama under protest, grinned delightedly at the joke. She was going into fourth grade, and beginning to feel as if she'd be grown-up any minute. All summer she had talked about cutting off her waist-long braids.

Watching her, Sally thought with amusement that Betsy's braces were almost becoming. If she'd realized that braces were, well, kind of cute, like that, she wouldn't have made such a fuss over her own.

"Couldn't you find Rick?" Mrs. Burnaby identified the empty place. "Sometimes I wonder if that boy will ever learn to tell time!"

"He said he was just going to ride down to school and see what it looked like," Jimmy volunteered virtuously.

Sally grinned at him affectionately. He was the sweetest little brother you could ask for, with his round freckled face, mussed hair, and missing front teeth — so angelic-looking above the neck, and so tough-looking below, in the striped jersey and blue jeans. He sat so close to his plate that his table manners were not very noticeable, and he had learned at an early age not to call attention to himself unless the occasion was sure to draw a laugh.

Dad looked at the empty chair thoughtfully but said nothing. Just as he handed Sally her plate, the culprit arrived.

"Well, imagine seeing you here!" observed Jean. Ricky glared at her, as he slid into his chair. He looked much as Jimmy would at twelve when he had all his teeth again: a crew-cut cherub, with big blue eyes

[17]

alert to the storm signals that seemed to be flying in his direction most of the time.

"Gee, mom — that clock down on Main Street said only quarter to six. How should I know it was six thirty?"

"That clock has never kept time in all the years we've lived here. Where's your watch?"

The watch had been wrung from a dubious family in the hope that it might improve Ricky's punctuality.

Ricky faced six pairs of eyes engagingly, trying to camouflage his uneasiness with nonchalance, relying on his familiar technique of clowning to disarm them. He looked at his mother with an impish twinkle that invited her to laugh.

"Well, I kinda suspected mebbe it was getting time for supper," he said, as if *everybody* knew how that was, illustrating his story with exaggerated gestures. "I said to the boys, 'Hey, fellas, how's about going home?' And they all said to me: 'What you talking about? It's only four o'clock!'" His glance wavered over to his father's attentive face, and for a moment his confidence was shaken. Then he pulled himself together and went on. "So I pulled up the old sleeve to see for myself, and what do you know?" He paused dramatically, and Jean's dimple betrayed irresistible amusement. "It wasn't there!" He waved his hands helplessly. "What could I do? There I was on second base — one out, one on first, score tied — and then — "

"A remarkable story," commented his father without a trace of amusement, "but I think we've heard enough. Where is the watch?"

"Well," Ricky was still playing for a break, "I figure I musta left it in my bag. It wasn't running right last night, and I just stuck it in with my underwear. But

[18]

you can see how I was late."

"What I can see," pursued his father relentlessly, "is that you're starting just where you left off before the trip. Well — we're through. From here on, beginning tonight, if you can't get to supper on time you eat in the kitchen."

Ricky carried his plate on an upraised hand at a level with the top of his head, set his other arm akimbo, and swung jauntily through the kitchen door with an acquiescent, "Aye, aye, sir!"

Sally giggled as the door swung behind him, and Jean smiled her rare, contagious smile, glancing at her father to enjoy the joke with her. But he wasn't having any tonight.

"The whole trouble, Sara," he addressed himself severely to his wife, "is that everyone laughs at Ricky. You girls are old enough to know better! Next time we'll cut out his dessert."

Sally subsided in shocked silence. It would hurt all of them to see Ricky deprived of dessert! The telephone rang and Sally jumped up. Suddenly she remembered Kate's news.

"I hope someone will enjoy this year," she remarked pessimistically, as she left the table. "I know I won't!"

Her mother looked surprised.

"I'll hate it too," said Jean gloomily.

Dad began to look unsettled. "What's wrong?" he asked Jean.

"Just school! Joyce is in everything — I never see her any more, and I'm no good at organizations. Everybody is doing something but me. It's awful!"

Dad looked a little relieved. "How about the teachers?"

Jean shrugged. "Oh, they're all right. I don't mind

[19]

the studying. It's just that left-out feeling. And I can't do anything about it."

"Maybe this year will be different," mother tried to reassure her. "Now you're a sophomore, you know more what to expect."

"Yeah, I know more — and all of it's worse." Jean refused the assurance.

"I'm feeling good about school!" Ricky announced from the kitchen. "But I sure don't feel good about math! If I had a dog now — "

"Oh, for goodness' sake!" Mother rose abruptly and began clearing the table. "Once and for all, Rick, there will be no dog in this house until you show some sign of responsibility! You needn't even mention him again, until you grow up!"

Rick sighed the long sigh of the unreasonably persecuted.

"O.K., mom!" he agreed, "but I betcha I get the pooch yet!"

"That I will have to see," she told him firmly.

Jean finished clearing the table, mother served the ice cream and frozen raspberries, Jimmy spilled a large gob of fruit on his fresh mat, apologized with a silent angelic smile, and dinner was over.

"For heaven's sake," said Mr. Burnaby with weary patience, "tell Sally to cut it short! Fifteen minutes is enough! She's going down there tonight, isn't she?"

"Kate, I've got to go now," said Sally, anticipating the parental order. "I'll come down soon's the dishes are done."

"Mother!" She ate her ice cream in snatches as she helped dry the dishes. "I've simply got to tell you — "

"Ricky is not to go out tonight." Mr. Burnaby came out into the kitchen carrying one milky glass. "If he

[20]

hasn't enough sense to come in, we'll just keep hold of him while we've got him! "

" O dad! " Ricky wailed. " Daylight savings goes off in a couple of weeks — this is just about my last chance! "

" It's just about your last chance to come in on time too," said his father imperturbably. " Try it again tomorrow. When you get to supper on time, you go out afterward — not otherwise."

Ricky looked dashed. Argument with his father was useless. It didn't get you far with mother, either, but at least you could carry it on with some spirit for a while, and it could be entertaining. He went soberly into the sunroom and sprawled on the floor with the evening newspapers.

" I was talking to Kate," Sally began again, " and — "

" Do you want the rest of the raspberries in the icebox, or can I just eat them up? " asked Jean hopefully.

" Eat them up," said Mrs. Burnaby, splashing the silver through the suds. Without warning she remembered Sally's last words.

" What's all this about Kate? " she asked suddenly. " Why don't you just tell us without all the build-up? "

Sally took a deep breath. Why didn't she!

" She's going away to school this year! "

" Oh, for goodness' sake! " Jean had always claimed that if she could just go away to school everything would be different for her.

" I never thought the Kennicotts would send Kate away! " said mother, satisfactorily surprised.

" Well, her aunt left her a little legacy and specified that Kate was to have a year at Harper. Kate doesn't know whether she'll like it or not, but she sounded pretty excited." Sally was aggrieved.

"I think that's nice for Kate," said her mother.

"Nice for Kate, yes! But what about me?"

"Oh, you'll get along all right," said her mother, wiping up the sink and hanging cloths to dry. "It might be good for you not to depend on Kate so much."

That's how it always was, Sally thought bitterly. No one cared how she felt at all. All through high school she and Kate had done things together. And now Kate wouldn't be there for senior year.

What about the crowd? The double dates for dances and movies? And the football games! It would be no fun at all to go to them alone. Even the lunch hours! There were lots of other girls. But there wasn't anyone else like Kate.

Bleakly Sally faced herself in the mirror. She was going to be on her own this year. And what on earth was she going to do?

CHAPTER
TWO

⊱⊱⊰

H IGH SCHOOL *wasn't* the same without Kate. There was the same gay crowd in the halls, the same excited gossip, but none of it seemed important without Kate to share it. Sally missed her coming out of the classrooms, going to hockey, and especially on the way home. Warmed-over news in letters was highly unsatisfactory. Without Kate, Sally felt as if she'd had an amputation.

Now, on a Wednesday afternoon, she waited for Jean a little forlornly. The other girls were busy with orchestra and physical training and dramatics and boys. This year Sally couldn't make up her mind to enter the orchestra or chorus again — what was the use?

She still went to the Dairy Soda Bar on Monday afternoons when the rest of the gang went in for cokes. At least for the past two or three Mondays, someone had seen her after school and said: " Hi, Sally. Wanta get a coke? " She had gone along, feeling like a fifth wheel. Now she was beginning to wonder why she bothered.

" Hi, Sally! " Millie Davis stopped beside her with a cordial smile and Sally greeted her warmly. She had never cared for Millie when Kate was around. Millie lived on Juniper Lane too, next door to Kate, but she had been away at school until this year and Sally had seen her only occasionally during vacations.

She was a dramatic blonde, a year older than Sally, with shining long hair floating to her shoulders, knowing blue eyes, and clothes that seemed to call too much attention to her figure. When she was with Millie, as she seemed to be so often these days, Sally was uncomfortably aware of winks and nudges among the groups of boys in the halls.

"Going home now?" Millie asked.

"Soon as Jean comes along," Sally replied.

"I'll go along with you," Millie offered, with a glance around the hall. She smiled and waved at two or three boys who went by, and they grinned back, but made no effort to join the girls.

Jean appeared then, her arms full of books, looking bleak and discontented. Sally felt irritated. When she was in a good humor, there was something sparkly and fresh about Jean, an elusive charm that surprised Sally every time she noticed it. Jean's mouth was lovely when she smiled, but for her schoolmates that was seldom. They knew her only as she was now, sulky and plain.

"Joyce is staying for club," Jean said, her mouth drooping expressively. "I never see her any more."

"Why don't you join her club?" Sally asked.

"I loathe clubs," said Jean flatly. "If that's what Joyce wants to do, O.K. with me."

Sally had to admit that Jean was more independent about Joyce than she would have been. She had joined any activity with Kate and enjoyed them all.

"There's the cutest boy in my history class," Millie confided, as they climbed on the bus together. "I think he's new this year, and the minute I saw him I said, 'He's for me!' Honestly, he's wonderful!"

"Did he speak to you?" Sally was interested in how Millie managed these things.

"Not yet," said Millie, with an apologetic toss of her golden head. "But he will tomorrow! First thing you know we're walking out of class together — and the next thing you know he's taking me to a prom."

Sally had to admire her confidence. Luckily, she herself had Scotty to depend on. Last year he had taken her to some of the dances, and a couple of movies with Kate and Ted. Once or twice a boy in her class had called for a date. But it had always happened when she was going to be busy with Kate or the gang. No one had called for months, and she hadn't thought much about it until now.

She was thinking over Millie's nonchalant plan — if a boy walked out of class with you, how did you maneuver the prom? Just then she caught the expression on Jean's face: fascinated and disapproving.

"Of course," Millie sounded flatteringly respectful, "you've got Scotty. I think he's terribly cute, and so kind of indifferent — don't you get a big kick out of going with the son of a Congressman?"

"Well — " Sally had never considered Scotty in that light before. They had been friends since fourth grade, and George Stephenson Scott, Sr., had gone to Congress for only one term, before they had graduated from grammar school, and then had been defeated and returned to his law business. She'd almost forgotten about it, and Scotty never mentioned it at all.

"I don't know if I actually go with him," she said, "at least not steady."

"Well, I certainly would," said Millie with conviction. "You could, you know. He's simply mad about you."

Sally could almost feel Jean's eyebrows raising. She

[25]

had not the slightest reason to think Scotty was mad about her, but it was pleasant to hear it. Only, how did you manage going steady?

"Look," Millie lowered her voice to a confidential tone, "everybody knows he's never gone with another girl. And he's at your house as often as not. Eddie told me that Red told him that Don said he heard Scotty say he thought you were quite a girl. So you see?"

"Uh-huh," agreed Sally, with a warm feeling inside. She looked up at Jean, who was staring through the window.

The bus drew up at Fourth Street and the three girls jumped off and sauntered up Juniper Lane together. The Burnaby house was the third from the corner, a friendly white frame house with green trim and a big screened porch across the front and side. Millie waved good-by as Sally and Jean turned in at their walk. Her own square stucco house was three doors away, and she walked along as if she had a camera trained on her.

Jean dropped her books on the porch table and made an expressive gesture with her hands, rolling her eyes.

"Good night, she's worse than ever!"

"Oh, I don't know," Sally defended her new friend. "She's really pretty popular. I thought she was kind of amusing."

"Funny is the word!" said Jean with a scathing inflection. "She's just a dope! Don't let her give you all that stuff about Scotty!"

"Well — " it was like cold water in her face, but Sally recovered and pretended indifference — "it would be nice if true. I never liked her much — but I thought today she wasn't as bad as I expected. At least she isn't snippy to girls who aren't popular — like us!"

Jean was already deep in a new magazine, and Sally

picked up her books and went on inside to find a cold drink. The day was warm for early October, and she found ginger ale in the icebox, fixed a glass with ice cubes for herself and, on second thought, one for Jean, and carried them back to the porch.

"Thanks," muttered Jean, without lifting her eyes from the page.

Sally sprawled on the glider, saddle shoes braced against the grass rug, and watched the quiet street. The trees drooped golden fringes above the sidewalk, and an occasional flurry of yellow leaves spilled onto the lawn. Children were coming home from the grade school.

Jimmy marched into the house, tough with first-grade importance.

"Hello, small fry," grinned Sally. "What's the big news at Juniper?"

"I can't read yet," he reported solemnly. Sally made round eyes at him. "Not yet?" she said in astonishment.

"Nope!" He stuck his hands on his hips and swaggered off to find his football, disillusioned with education.

Betsy rode up on her bike, dismounted, and went in the back door to the kitchen to find some food. Scotty was getting off the late high-school bus.

"Hi, Scotty! Ginger ale?" Sally shouted. Jean didn't move as Scotty came up the steps in two long strides and banged through the screen door.

"Hi, Burnaby," he said. "You've got the right idea. Where's the drink?"

"Out in the icebox, chump! Where'd you think?" his hostess told him amiably. He favored her with a grimace and swung through the house, which was as familiar to

[27]

him as his own. Filling the tallest glass he could find, he returned and plumped on the glider beside Sally, shaking her glass so that the liquid spilled on her skirt.

"Fathead!" she said, with violent scorn, mopping it up with a piece of kleenex. He grinned impishly, letting her know it was retaliation for making him get his own

drink. Jean began to giggle over the story she was reading.

Scotty was medium tall, stocky and confident, with an engaging grin full of teeth. Mindful of Millie's confidences, Sally looked at him as if she had never seen him before.

"How's school on the sophomore level?" he inquired of Jean.

She raised level gray eyes without smiling, and took a long drink of ginger ale.

"Terrible," she said.

"That's tough," he commented. "What's wrong?"

Jean set her glass down with an emphatic whack.

"Everything," she said, "except, of course, the teachers. And they're not so good either. I don't mind classes — much. But Joyce is in a million activities and I never see her any more, and nobody speaks to me hardly — and I loathe hockey! And everybody is always talking about people I don't know! There ought to be an easier way to get an education."

Scotty nudged Sally with a loose elbow and waved his glass at Jean.

"She doesn't like it," he elucidated. Sally giggled.

"I guess she doesn't," she agreed. "That's what she's been saying for quite a while now." Jean had already gone back to her magazine.

"Well," said Scotty, finding his sophomore audience had stopped listening, "tell your sister from an old-timer that them as has gits."

Jean looked at him with mingled interest and scorn.

"A girl with her nose in a book all the time isn't going to find the crowd digging her out to show her a time." He stated it with a placid lack of emphasis and drained his glass, tinkling the ice cubes against his teeth as he extracted one to suck. "Furthermore, maybe if she spoke to someone, they'd speak to her, and after a while she'd know all these people the other people talk about."

"Going to the game Saturday?" he asked Sally.

"Sure. Are you?"

"Yep. Maybe I'll see you there. How about a movie Saturday night?"

"That would be wonderful!" Sally made an extra effort to show him how much she would like it, and he looked somewhat startled.

[29]

"O.K., see you then. Jean, you listen to Uncle George and you'll be O.K. Are you going to the game?"

Jean scowled a little. "I don't know. I might. But it'd be more of what I get at school all the time."

"Maybe you'd like the team to come play in your front yard so you could read a book while you watched them?"

Jean had to grin, that sudden unexpected, twinkly smile that always caught people by surprise and made them look at her twice.

"All right, Uncle George! I'll go this time. But I'm warning you — if that team doesn't give me cold chills, I'm not wasting my time again."

"I'll speak to the captain myself," said Scotty gravely. "He's an old friend of mine, and I know he'd do anything for me."

He cut across the yard, whistling as he went. Sally watched him with amusement. He was pretty cute at that. She never got bored with him. Maybe Millie was right about going steady with him.

It didn't cross her mind that Scotty might have his own opinions on that subject.

CHAPTER
THREE

SINCE Wednesday, when Scotty had suggested the Saturday-night date, Sally had hardly seen him at all. That was not surprising. Scotty was a busy boy, opening his campaign for class office, swimming two afternoons a week, singing another afternoon with the chorus.

Jean had decided to sing in the chorus this year too. She explained, with a disclaiming shrug, that her teacher told her she ought to be doing something, and she guessed she might as well make it something musical. Sally had almost made up her mind to join when she heard that Scotty was singing. But it seemed like an awful lot of trouble, when she could see Scotty other ways. She thought about it for a month, and then let it go by default.

Now that she had determined to concentrate on his steady company, Sally noticed his absences more than she ever had. She looked for him in the halls, watched for him to go past the house (he never stopped in now), and even wondered if he would keep the date.

That was silly too; their dates had always been casual, and he had always kept them. Nor had he ever dated another girl, all the time she had known him. Millie reminded her of that, when Sally confided to her on Thursday afternoon that she was going out with him.

"What did you want to tell her for?" asked Jean contemptuously. "She'll spread it all over the school."

"There's nothing wrong with that, is there?" Sally snapped.

Jean shrugged in her maddening manner, implying "terribly stupid, but I wouldn't say so for anything," and Sally felt vaguely uncomfortable. But she had to talk to someone, and when she was with Millie it just seemed to slip out. She had almost asked if Millie was going to the game, but had caught that back in time. She didn't want Millie along — especially if Jean was going.

Taking Jean to her first football game was kind of fun. At least it took Sally's mind off Kate's absence. She was so anxious to have Jean like it that she kept explaining to her about all the players and all the plays, until Jean said violently, "Keep still and let me just look at it!"

Sally was worrying Jean into being contrary, just as mother told her she did. A little sulkily she concentrated on the game and paid no more attention to her sister. And to her surprise, she forgot about her own troubles when the Sherwood team completed a long pass in the third quarter and ran for the touchdown.

After that Jean was sold, and Sally could relax. She was amazed at how fast Jean understood the game. When she was a freshman she had been foggy most of the year over what football was all about. But then, Jean was smart. Sally looked at her, concentrating intensely on the play. It was kind of surprising the way you could find things out about your sister, if you thought a little. Jean seemed a lot older than a sophomore in some ways. Maybe she was growing up.

The excitement had died down for a minute, and

Sally looked over the stands for Scotty. He was in his usual place, with no thought of looking for her. She waved her pennant wildly, but there was no response. It didn't matter. Tonight was the night.

Jean said little about the game, which Sherwood won, 14–6. She didn't care to go to the Ranch House where the crowd usually gathered afterward. But Sally didn't mind; she was anxious to get home and begin getting ready for the evening.

They both walked home in silence. And then Jean surprised Sally by saying, "Maybe it would be a good idea if I learned how to curl my hair."

"It's about time," Sally said, with all the pleasure of one who has told you so. "I'll do it up for you the minute we get home. And I'll show you how to put on some nail polish too. You could really look very nice, if you made the effort, Jean."

"Maybe," said Jean indifferently. It hit Sally like a cold wind that she had lost the sale. She opened her mouth, thought better of it, and closed it again. Surely she hadn't been nagging this time! But Jean was so touchy.

Feeling grossly misjudged, Sally didn't say another word about it all the way home. Nor did Jean, who buried herself in a book as soon as she got inside the door.

But when Sally was dressing for her date, Jean watched her closely, asking no questions, making no remarks. Just watching. And this time Sally was careful not to say anything instructive.

She looked over her dresses thoughtfully: it had to be something special. Finally she chose the aqua jersey with the sunburst of nailheads at the throat, and the wide silver belt. She brushed out her hair again, straightened her stocking seams, retouched her lips, added the charm bracelet on which every charm meant something special. Scotty had given her an oar, with a note about paddling her own canoe, for her last birthday.

The doorbell rang, and she looked in the mirror again. She had never made a point of coming down after Scotty arrived. All the other times he was just the boy down the street, but tonight she was going to make an entrance.

Downstairs she could hear her family chattering with him. Repressing a slight quiver, Sally descended.

" Hi-ya, Sal! " Scotty pulled himself lazily to his feet. It wasn't a very romantic opening, but Sally looked at him intensely and tried to convey the idea that he was very important. He looked past her without meeting her eyes. " Ready for the show? " He held out one hand to help her with her coat. Maybe he was self-conscious about the family.

After she had climbed in, he closed the door of his car with a rattly slam, and stepped over the door on the other side. Sally leaned back and laid her head on the leather upholstery, turning a little to watch Scotty at the wheel.

The aged Chevrolet convertible was Scotty's pride and joy. He had worked hard, since eighth grade, with newspaper routes, egg routes, and summer jobs, to earn the money to buy it last spring. Now he was still working hard to earn the money to run it. He pampered it and talked about it like a fond parent.

Now he leaned an anxious ear beyond the windshield.

" Hear that funny kind of gasp in the motor? " he asked.

Sally sat up and listened.

" No."

"Well, it must be all right. I had her all apart after the game this afternoon, and she was purring like a kitten when I came over tonight."

"She sounds good to me." If he wanted to spend the whole evening talking about his car, Sally would try to keep up with him.

"I love this car," she said, "and you take wonderful care of it."

"It gets around," he said carelessly. "Jean like the game this afternoon?"

"She seemed to," said Sally. "I thought it was swell."

Scotty nodded, eyes on the road.

"She'll get along," he said. "If she just doesn't decide all the time she'd rather read. If you want to be someone around high school, you have to do it for yourself."

"I guess so," agreed Sally. "I notice it without Kate. It takes more effort to do things alone. Even the gang isn't the same."

"They're the same. You aren't." Scotty was frank. "You act like the person you're with, and now it seems to be Millie."

"What's wrong with Millie?" Sally was defensive.

Scotty shrugged.

"Nothing special. Only she isn't your type. And she thinks all the boys are crazy about her, and they aren't. At least not the fellows I know."

"Don't you think she's awfully pretty?"

"Oh, pretty!" For the first time he looked at Sally directly and looked away again. "Maybe — but that has nothing to do with it."

They were pulling into a parking space.

"What picture are we seeing?"

"That new musical show at the Plaza. O.K.?"

"O.K."

It was kind of hard to make much progress in the movie house. Scotty slouched in his seat, guffawing at the picture as if Sally didn't exist. She liked it too, but her mind was divided.

When they came out, she stumbled on the tiled floor and clutched his arm. Without a word Scotty set her firmly on her feet and moved on out of the movie house as if her stumble were no concern of his.

"Soda?"

How could you think a boy was taking an interest in you, if he didn't even notice when you nearly broke your ankle? A little uncertainly Sally followed him into the Dairy Soda Bar. At least, over a table, they might be able to talk. He hadn't met her eyes all evening – except once, and then he didn't look as if he liked her.

She saw a table for two and started toward it, just as Scotty saw four of the gang sitting at a big table with two empty places.

"There's some of the crowd," he said, turning toward them. They couldn't even sit alone! Sally accepted it with good grace, and sat across from him, where she could watch him. But Scotty didn't seem to see her. He was having a wonderful time, joking with the boys, and teasing the girls.

It was all the way it used to be – with a difference. Before, Sally had enjoyed herself. She had liked Scotty just the way he was – easygoing and indifferent and effortless. Now something was missing. She had a feeling he was trying to avoid her.

On the way home, Sally made a last effort.

"We've always had fun, haven't we? All the way through high school, I mean. And here we are seniors."

"Uh-huh." Scotty was listening for that noise in the motor again.

"This ought to be our big year. Only — without Kate I haven't been so sure."

"You'll get along. Just be yourself."

No response in his voice. No appreciative glance.

"I guess so." Sally wasn't sure at all any more. "Are you going to Marian's next Saturday?"

"Well — I might be busy." Too busy for a party with the crowd? "But they're all coming to my house the week after. You coming?" It was a question, not an invitation.

"Why, of course! We have more fun at your house than anywhere!"

She made that full of meaning.

Scotty said, "That's good."

The car stopped in front of her house, and Scotty climbed over the door again. The latch was stubborn, and he avoided opening it when he could. Sally waited until he opened her door.

"How about a sandwich?" she asked. Their dates had always ended with a session in the kitchen.

"Thanks. Gotta run. Swell evening. Be seeing you."

He was gone before she could say anything more. Something was all wrong, and Sally had no idea what it was.

D RESSING for the Sherwood-Clinton football
game, Sally was surprised at how much she was
looking forward to it. It was two weeks now since she
had talked to Scotty. Not since their date. She couldn't
believe that he was avoiding her. Of course, he had so
many things to do, with his job, and his car, and his
swimming, and so on.

Sally furrowed her brow, trying to remember the
times she had seen him at school. Once in the cafeteria
line, when he had said, " Hi, Sal! " as if he barely knew
her. And that time she had seen him talking to a new
girl outside the chemistry lab.

Suppose he was going to date someone else! Sally almost dropped her hairbrush at the idea. But he had
never gone with anyone but her. What on earth would
she do?

She began brushing again, with long, violent strokes.
During the last couple of weeks she had thought about
Scotty so much that she had forgotten to wonder what
Kate would do. This was something she would have to
figure out for herself. She hadn't mentioned her problem
to Millie, feeling that putting it into words might jell
the situation the wrong way. Try to forget it, she
thought. It'll come out all right.

She pinned her hair back with more than usual attention. Perhaps she would see Scotty at the game, or at

the Ranch House afterward. Then she chose a fresh pair of jeans and a clean aqua T-shirt, and tied a scarlet ribbon in her hair.

She turned from the mirror as Jean came into the room. "Aren't you going to fix up a little? "

Jean looked obdurate, as she always did at Sally's suggestions.

" I'm all right the way I am. Nobody is going to notice me."

" Well, at least you could try this lipstick. It ought to be exactly right on you. See! "

Jean pulled away in annoyance. " When I want to wear lipstick I'll put it on myself, for heaven's sake! Now let me alone! "

At least Jean's hair was looking better now. Last week end she had finally tried putting it up in pin curls, and she was as pleased with the result as Sally herself. Sally had remembered to be tactful and not suggest further improvements just then. But the time always came when she couldn't stand Jean's appearance another minute.

" Are you going to the Ranch House afterward with us? "

Jean considered with a shrug. " I might. I don't know. Will you be meeting the boys? "

" They might be there," said Sally, who felt that was the only reason for going herself. " If you are coming, you ought at least to wear lipstick."

"Well, I can always put it on later."

Sally gave up. It was hopeless to work on Jean until she felt an impulse of her own.

Sally had to admit the attitude had certain admirable qualities. She herself was more suggestible, depending on her friends for ideas and initiative, and weighing what they would think before she acted. Jean didn't care at all what people thought. If they didn't agree with her, she labeled them dopes and forgot about them.

Kate was like Jean, Sally thought, only more tactful — that was what made her a leader. Kate's ideas for parties and games were always good; she was the one, for instance, who had started the crowd learning to rumba and tango when jitterbugging began to go out. The gang was gathering at Scotty's house tonight, the first real get-together since school started. Kate's absence would make quite a hole.

As she started down the street with Jean, Sally's spirits lifted. The October sky was a brilliant blue, and a crisp little breeze ruffled her hair. She scuffed along, enjoying the hollow whisper of the dried leaves underfoot, watching one golden leaf after another slowly spiral down. It was a perfect day for the game!

The other girls were already in their usual places in the bleachers when Sally and Jean arrived: Becky Horton, petite and blond and sparkling, with big brown eyes; and Marian Lord, whose naturally curly red hair tumbled all over the place, and who talked in such enthusiastic superlatives that everyone had to listen to her. They waved and squealed and crowded together to make room for Sally and Jean.

"Isn't this marvelous?" cried Marian, as the Burnabys sat down. "Look, there are the boys over there!" She waved her pennant across the stands and sat down bouncily. Sally stared eagerly, caught sight of Scotty's red hair, and waved too. Marian was still chattering. "Glen says the party tonight is going to be out of this world. There's going to be a new girl too! She can't take Kate's place — but at least we'll be even couples."

"What is she like?" asked Sally, immediately curious.

"Nobody seems to know," said Marian, looking at her

[40]

with an odd expression. Sally didn't much care. She'd see her tonight.

"Well, come on!" shouted Becky to the team coming onto the field. "What are we waiting for? Let's get going!"

Jean was watching eagerly as the teams trotted out, fastening their helmets, and prancing up and down to limber their muscles. This was one of the tightest games on the Sherwood schedule. But it wouldn't have mattered. Jean had discovered football, and every game was important. By now she knew each of the players by name, and she chattered about them like an old-timer. Sally threw her an occasional glance and relaxed. She wouldn't have to worry about Jean and football any longer.

The ball went into play and the game began. From the beginning it was obvious that the Sherwood team outweighed the Clinton boys. Even so, the visitors were putting up a strong enough fight so that the Sherwood stands grew tense with emotion.

Then in the second quarter it happened. Sherwood had attempted to pass twice and Clinton had intercepted. Jean was digging her nails into her palms. Sally was leaning forward, grimly willing the team to make the down. The stands expected Sherwood to kick: they were on their own thirty-yard line and couldn't afford to lose any more ground. The team fell back into kicking position, feinted the ball, and unexpectedly passed, quarter to halfback, to fullback, who started running along the side of the field with expert interference.

The crowd came to their feet, howling with delight. Sherwood had made their down and the fullback was still running. At the fifty-yard line a Clinton back blocked the interference, and two others tackled the fullback heavily. Everyone in the stands could see the fury behind the tackle. The fullback hit the ground, still hugging the ball, and lay much too quiet. The spectators broke into an uproar of indignation and then hushed, waiting.

Sally was watching the whole business closely: the water boys ran out, the doctor ran out, the coaches clustered over the still figure. Finally the fullback was hauled to his feet, holding his head, and was led stumbling off the field. The substitute ran in and the game went on.

"Aren't they even going to penalize those thugs?" Sally demanded of Becky, who nudged her and gestured toward Jean. Sally looked over her shoulder. Jean, white as paper, was watching the fullback as he staggered toward the bench and was led back to the showers.

"What's the matter, Jean? Don't you feel well?" Sally asked.

Jean shook her head with an agonized expression. "Sally, do you think he's hurt badly? I've just got to know!"

Sally stared in amazement. "What on earth's the matter? It was a rough tackle, and Clinton was penalized five yards. And Hank Miller — he was hurt, I guess, but he walked off the field."

"If it had been anyone but Hank!" Jean moaned. "I can't stand it — to see him mauled like that before my eyes!"

The light dawned. Jean had a crush on Hank Miller, Sherwood's star fullback! Jean — with a crush! Sally couldn't believe it, but she had a sudden sensation that she'd lived through all this before. She remembered the time she herself had a freshman crush on the football captain and had felt for a couple of months just the way

Jean did now. She reached for her sister's hand, feeling for the first time as if they had something in common.

"I know just how it is," she assured her. "Why, Jean — I had no idea — Hank Miller! My goodness!"

"I didn't intend to fall for a football star," Jean was close to tears, "but he's so big and kind of modest and you'd never know he's the best player on the team. He walks out just like any one of the players. And they all admire him. You can just tell. He's simply wonderfull And then those — those brutes had to hit him like that —"

Marian leaned across with a comforting pat.

"I know he'll be all right, Jean. When they can walk off the field, it's not too bad. And he'll be in school Monday, bet you anything."

"Did you feel this way at all the games?" Sally was keenly interested in this unforeseen development. Jean shook her head forlornly.

"I don't know how I missed it before!" she confessed. "But I kind of noticed him last week, especially — and today it just sort of hit me!"

Moodily she watched the substitute fullback, who was unquestionably inferior, sure that the game must be lost now that Hank Miller was out. The whistle blew for the half with the score tied.

The band marched out, rhythmic and colorful, the best high-school band in the state. The stands rose for the Sherwood song and again for the Clinton song. Pennants waved, popcorn dropped like snow, peanuts crunched under foot. Down in front of the bleachers, the cheerleaders were turning cart wheels in their blue and orange school colors and pulling the audience through locomotive cheers, ending with leaps that would have graced a ballet.

"I'll bet it was a brain injury," Jean was brooding. "He probably won't play again this season, and it's his senior year!"

"They never get hurt that badly," Sally said optimistically. "He's in my English class — I just remembered."

"Oh! For heaven's sake! Tell me all about him. I had no idea you knew him!"

Privately Sally had always considered Hank Miller as rather dull and unattractive, but not for worlds would she have told that to Jean.

"Why," she began slowly, trying to think of the right things to say, "he's all right, I guess. The teacher seems to think he's pretty funny." That was accurate enough. The teacher spent innumerable sarcasms on the literary light of the football team, who never even recognized them. "I don't think he's getting the best marks," Sally went on cautiously, "but of course he's *passing!*"

Jean had always maintained that high marks were what you went to high school for. But now she nodded in approval.

"He's doing something else so important it wouldn't be surprising if his English came second. After all, grades aren't everything, do you think?"

Sally gulped. Maybe this change of attitude was healthy. "No, they certainly aren't everything. In fact, that's what Scotty and I have been trying to tell you."

Jean missed that. The team was returning to the field, and she clutched Sally's arm with frantic fingers. "Sally! Look! He's coming back with the team!" Sure enough, Hank Miller was trotting out on the field, adjusting his helmet as if nothing had happened. Jean sat back completely happy.

The two teams fought bitterly through the second

half, and Sally found herself watching the fullback more than the rest of the team. She couldn't see anything especially thrilling about him, or outstanding about his playing. But she knew from experience that when That Feeling hit you there was no accounting for it.

Sherwood lost. The final score was 21–20.

"Oh, well," said Jean philosophically, as they began to climb down from the stands, "after all, Hank couldn't win the game singlehanded, when the rest of the team made so many errors. The score would have been twice as bad without him." Sally thought of Kate, for the first time since the half. She had enjoyed this game almost as much as if Kate had been there!

They rounded the corner of the bleachers as the team were going into the locker rooms. "Sally," Jean hissed in her ear, "there he is!!!"

There he was, dirty and sagging in his muddy football suit, a trickle of blood on his chin, his shoulders dragging with exhaustion. Jean stood still and a miracle happened. Hank looked directly toward the crowd, saw Sally, and grinned fuzzily.

" Isn't he simply wonderful! " Jean sighed. " Sally, he smiled at you! Oh, I can hardly wait till Monday! "

" What about the Ranch House? " Sally felt kind of excited about Jean's situation. And Jean looked almost pretty when she forgot about herself like this. With an unaccustomed gesture, Jean's hand went up to her hair.

" All right," she agreed. " Does the team come in? "

" Sometimes," said Sally. " Not always. But it is kind of fun."

Jean looked undecided. Then she grinned. " Give me your lipstick," she said, with a twinkle in her eye at the joke on herself.

CHAPTER
FIVE

⋙⋙⋙⋙⋙⋙⋙⋙⋙⋙⋙⋙⋙⋙⋙⋙⋙⋙⋙⋙⋙⋙

SALLY sat alone in the corner of Scotty's recreation room trying to figure it out. She'd looked forward to this evening for days, and at ten o'clock she was ready to go home.

Becky Horton was playing ping-pong with Bill Nixon. Glen Fowler was beating out hot music on the old piano. Marian was jitterbugging with Ted Frith. Sally's lip curled at that. Hardly anyone jitterbugged any more.

Scotty was sitting in another corner, talking to Louise Buck.

That was what Sally couldn't figure out. The rest of them, and Kate, had danced and played and gone to games and movies together since they were freshmen. Some girl they all knew and liked had filled in from time to time, when Sally had the flu, or Becky was sick, or Marian was out of town. But why Louise this time? None of the girls knew her.

Watching her with narrowed eyes, Sally didn't think much of the idea. Louise was a gentle-looking girl, with smooth brown hair and big brown eyes, and a shy way of looking helpless and getting taken care of. By ten thirty Sally had to admit that it was Scotty who was taking care of her.

All the others knew their way around Scotty's recreation room as well as their own houses. They ought to: the gang had helped Scotty decorate it two years ago when his folks told him he could have the space. It was a fairly large room, well furnished now, with a sofa, chairs, and several tables that his mother had discarded from upstairs. At one end was a kitchen arrangement, with a two-burner gas range for hot dogs and cocoa and popcorn, a long table space, and shelves full of supplies. Scotty had even found an old icebox and painted it. For occasions like this he stocked it with ice and milk.

Marian walked over to the icebox at the end of the dance, took out a bottle of ginger ale and one of grape juice, and mixed them with ice cubes in a big pitcher. Ted set out some glasses.

"Drinks coming up!" he bellowed. Marian cupped her hands around her mouth. "Who wants a sandwich?"

"Make mine peanut butter," said Bill Nixon. He was as lazy as Becky was energetic, and his favorite pose was that he was being pushed around. "I never believe in doing what I can get someone else to do for me!"

Sally had no appetite. She was watching Louise, who sat looking helpless and appealing until Scotty turned her way.

To Sally's chagrin, instead of saying, as he would have to her, "You've got feet, haven't you?" he went over to the counter, filled a glass, and spread a sandwich for Louise. She thanked him prettily as he sat down beside her.

When she spoke again, it was in such a confidential tone that he had to lean toward her, listening in a special manner that Sally had never noticed before. What was going on here?

With a jerk, Sally got out of her chair and went over

to the counter to make herself a sandwich and pour out some ginger ale and grape juice. Then she wandered over to watch Glen Fowler pound the piano. Usually she found his playing fascinating, but tonight it sounded just noisy.

"Who is this Louise Buck?" was on the tip of her tongue. But she decided no. After all, she knew who the girl was: a newcomer to Sherwood who had been around for some weeks now. In fact, she was in Sally's history class, and Sally had seen Scotty talking to her in the hall last week. She was afraid it was Scotty's idea to include her tonight.

"How about a dance?" demanded Glen, striking a couple of special chords to conclude his effort. He left the piano to look through the record rack.

"Something smooth," said Sally, feeling tired of jive.

Glen danced with a polished inventiveness, and Sally would have enjoyed it, except that the sentimental music only emphasized everything that was wrong with the evening. She saw Louise hold out her hands for Scotty to pull her up from the deep chair, and they walked out on the floor hand in hand as if they had a secret. Sally couldn't bear to watch them. Scotty had never looked at her like that.

Glen whispered understandingly, as the record stopped, "Watch me break this up!" He sauntered over, made a clownish bow from the waist, and nudged Louise's elbow. "Our dance, your highness!"

Louise looked up at Scotty as if she couldn't bear to leave him, and then turned radiantly to Glen, as if she were delighted. Even Glen acted as if he liked her, although he wasn't simpering like Scotty.

Scotty turned to Sally and, uneasily, she felt as if he did it because he had to. She was waiting for him to say,

"Where have you been all night?" But he didn't. He grinned easily, and led her expertly through some complicated steps, as if he could do all this in his sleep. But she could feel his attention on Glen and Louise.

"No flies on you, Sally," he said graciously as the music stopped.

"Thank you for the attention," she said acidly.

"Don't give it a thought," he advised her.

She rather expected him to dance with her again, but Louise looked over at that moment and said: "Scotty, this is the most wonderful room! Didn't you say you had some special records?"

Of course, Scotty was delighted to bring out his treasures, and, of course, Louise was right beside him, studying the collection, making remarks of appreciation that kept him listening to her alone. It was sickening. Sally wandered back to her armchair and picked up a book. Never in her life had she sat at a party and read!

Thank goodness, it was eleven thirty! Twelve o'clock was always the deadline for parties. Sally caught Becky's eye and suggested leaving. Becky announced in a voice like a train caller: "Party's over, folks! Dishes!"

"So soon?" said Louise in a dreamy voice. "I've had such fun I can't believe it's time to go home!" She helped Scotty put his records away and then sat down on the piano bench beside Glen.

Becky and Sally washed the dishes and picked up the kitchen. Scotty drifted around collecting glasses and plates, but his mind was not on his work. Glen seemed reluctant to leave the piano. Louise kept begging him for just one more song, and Scotty was so distracted by the music that he ended up hanging over the keyboard with the others. Even Ted was huddling over the piano. Sally felt affronted with the whole business. The cleanup was everybody's job, and the deadline was never delayed. By that time she was so cross she could hardly set the glasses down without banging them.

On an impulse she crossed the floor to the piano, determined to compete with Louise and wishing she had made up her mind to do it earlier.

"Scotty," she said, in a tone that told him and Louise that she was practically one of the family, "it's time we were leaving. Going on twelve, you know. Come on, now, and give us a hand with the cleanup!"

The expression in his eyes as he looked up at her startled her. *Why, he looks as if he hates me!* she thought in panic. *Now what have I done?*

The resentment faded and he grinned, the old familiar grin, but with a difference. "O.K., mom!" he conceded, with a wicked twinkle. "You sound just like my mother!" He left the piano, picked up the scattered things on the counter, and whisked a damp cloth along the top. Sally felt worse than ever. So she sounded like his mother, did she? That was practically fatal.

Gloomily she found her coat, wondering how to erase her error. Scotty was at the door with the crowd, and she laid her hand on his arm to claim his attention.

"Scotty, it was a wonderful party," she said, looking up brightly. "Did I really sound like your mother? It must just be because I know her so well. I didn't intend to give orders about your party — but —"

The apology faded out as Scotty reassured her without a smile.

"That's O.K., Sally. Probably a good thing you got us started. It really is time to break it up." She looked down at her hand on his sleeve. There wasn't much point in keeping it there, and she took it away, feeling futile and unhappy.

[51]

The next morning Sally woke up feeling as cross as when she had gone to bed. Jean was sitting at the dressing table, brushing her hair.

"What do you think of it?" she asked.

The pin curls had done their job. Jean's light-brown hair was soft and waving, full of lights, curling around her slender oval face. She grinned at Sally in the mirror, enchanted with the result.

"It's swell, Jean!" Sally sat up in bed, stretching and yawning, beginning to feel a little better. Something about Sunday morning made her feel good in spite of herself.

"Well," Jean was brushing it with loving care, pushing it into place, looking at the effect from all angles, "it seems like a lot of trouble. But now that I've discovered Hank — Sally!" She laid down the brush and turned to face her sister. "Do you think there's a chance of ever meeting him?"

"Could be," said Sally, without much encouragement in her voice. "You really think he's pretty cute?"

"He isn't at all handsome," said Jean with admirable frankness, "in fact, he's quite homely. But when you remember that wonderful pass he caught — and how heroic he was in all that pain, when he was knocked out — he's just too marvelous!"

"I guess so," said Sally.

"Was it a good party at Scotty's?" asked Jean.

"It was gruesome," said Sally, feeling depressed again. "There was this new girl, there — and — oh, I don't know. It was terrible."

Jean looked at her sister wisely. "Did she snare Scotty?"

"Well —" in the bright Sunday morning, the whole thing seemed like a silly nightmare. Sally sat up again and twined her arms about her knees. "He seemed sort of struck with her, I guess. I didn't like her at all, and it made the evening kind of dull."

Jean nodded as if she knew all about it. "I *thought* Millie was dumb," she remarked obscurely. "You didn't really care about Scotty, did you?"

"Not before," said Sally, climbing out of bed and thrusting her toes into woolly slippers. "I guess I don't anyway, only it took me by surprise. I'm kind of used to Scotty, and I don't know any other boys except the ones in the crowd, and they're all tied up."

"I wonder if Hank is going steady with anyone," Jean mused.

"I don't think so," Sally reassured her. She didn't think there was anyone who would care to go with Hank, but she didn't say so. A glance at the clock made her begin to hurry.

Like most of the high-school crowd, Sally and Jean never missed church. Ted and Scotty and Sally, and Kate when she was home, attended St. Paul's Episcopal Church. Jean sang in the choir, and the boys regularly served as crucifers and altar boys.

"Did you have a good time last night?" inquired Mrs. Burnaby, as the girls appeared for breakfast. She was enjoying her second cup of coffee with the book section of the paper in her hand. Dad liked to sleep late, and Jimmy and Betsy had already left for their own Sunday School service at nine thirty.

The electric percolator and toaster were on the sideboard, with a pile of bread and sweet rolls; orange juice and milk were on the table; bacon was hot in the oven.

"It was O.K.," said Sally vaguely. She pushed a slice of bread into the toaster, found the bacon, fried herself an egg. Last night was over and gone. Today was Sunday, and things might be entirely different.

Ricky came leaping downstairs as Jean left for choir, drank his orange juice in one gulp, swallowed a sweet roll and a piece of bacon, and ran out ahead of Sally. He was an acolyte this morning, and if he ran all the way he'd be on time.

Sally walked alone, loving the bright fall day. Beyond the black-limbed arch of trees the air was blue with the smoke of leaf fires. Jimmy and Betsy were coming home, gleaming with Sunday polish and white gloves. Sally smiled as they approached, waving story leaflets and dodging on and off the sidewalk in the old game of lines and squares. She could remember how long she had played the game every time she had walked down the street.

At the door of the church she saw Scotty and waved as casually as she could, hoping he had forgotten last night. Then she went on in to her regular place.

As the choir moved down the aisle behind the tall young crucifer, bearing the cross proudly high, Sally felt her troubles fade away. Church could always do that for her. The service and the prayers gave her peace and assurance and a sense of strength. She usually didn't keep the feeling for more than a day or so, but she could count on renewing it on Sunday.

Kneeling on the thick cushion, Sally tried to think charitably and kindly of Louise. The words of the general confession struck a penitential note that was comforting. As the priest pronounced the absolution, she felt for a few moments that she knew what was wrong with herself and what she should do. All she needed now was to go home and do it.

Her eyes wandered across the church: Scotty was in

his place. He caught her eye at that minute and grinned, as if they were still friends. Sally smiled back and then fixed her gaze on the altar. Last night didn't really matter after all.

The sermon was something about self-reliance, and Sally listened indifferently. But a few words the curate said registered in her mind like the echo of a bell: "You young folks have problems and sometimes the answers are hard to find. I repeat again the words of Christ: 'Ask, and it shall be given you; seek, and ye shall find; knock, and it shall be opened unto you.' That doesn't mean that He will give you whatever you ask, literally. It does mean that He will tell you what you need to know."

He went on, but Sally had stopped listening, turning over the words she had heard. Ask to have Scotty forget about Louise. That was no good. Seek to find out where she was making her mistake. The glowing exhilaration that swept through her meant that she was on the right track. She felt as if she could rearrange her life to order.

The service was over and the boys and girls streamed out, chattering outside the church, greeting each other with cheerful shouts. Sally was gay and exalted, full of confidence and good will. And then she saw Louise and Scotty standing together, her gloved hand on his arm, her appreciative manner meant only for him.

Well, really! That was the absolute edge. If Louise was going to go to St. Paul's, it was just going to spoil church for her, that was all! Sally seethed inside, as Jean inquired: "Who's that girl with Scotty? She's kind of cute!"

"Cute!" said Sally, in a choked voice, forgetting her prayers and inspiration. "Well — if you like that type! Let's go home!"

Home they went, Sally brooding upon the frustration of last night all over again. The nightmare hadn't faded after all.

"Are you going to Young Folks tonight?"

"I don't know," said Sally sulkily. "Why?"

"Oh, I just thought," said Jean, "it might be a good idea for me to go for a change."

Sally stared. Jean had always steadily declined to have anything to do with the Sunday evening high-school crowd at the church. Hank Miller was certainly changing her fast.

"Well" — Sally didn't want to go if Louise was going to be there, but on the other hand, if Jean was improving like this, Sally ought to show some interest — "well, I might as well."

Sally's high-school crowd liked the Young Folks Club on Sunday evenings. They liked the understanding young curate, they liked the entertainment, and they liked each other. It was a good way to spend Sunday evening.

Last year the crowd had collected for supper at one another's houses in turn, and each family had turned over the kitchen to them. They got together about five thirty for sandwiches and cocoa and fruit, and occasionally one of the girls provided a cake. By seven forty-five they all went to the parish house.

This year they had never got started on the suppers. That was because Kate wasn't there to round people up and start things off with the first meeting at her house, Sally was sure. She had gone to the meeting once, alone, but the next Sunday was cold and rainy and it didn't seem worth the effort to go out. After that it was easier to stay home.

By now Sally felt almost like a newcomer herself. As

seven thirty approached, she was more than half in-
clined to change her mind. But Jean was all ready to go,
and, feeling as if she were tagging after her sister, Sally
went with her.

When they got to the parish house, it was all right
after all. Same crowd, same music and laughter and
noisy fun. Sally drew a deep breath. It wasn't so hard
doing these things when you got started. Louise wasn't
there, she saw at once. Some boy she'd never seen before
came up and spoke to Jean. He was Jeff Sutton, in one
of Jean's classes, and they all sat together for the program.

A few minutes later Scotty sat down next to Sally. It
was the only vacant seat in the room. She smiled at him
and turned her attention to the chairman with a rush of
warm satisfaction. Scotty was his old self tonight, leaning back with his chin in the air and his hands in his
pockets, whispering an occasional joke to Sally or the
boy behind her. Sally felt entirely reassured.

It occurred to her that this was a good time to have
the gang over after the meeting. She turned the idea
over in her mind. Last year Kate would have made the
suggestion.

Well, if she was going to live a new life, no time like
the present to begin.

"Let's go to our house for food afterward," she suggested to Scotty. There was a shadow of hesitation in
his face. Then he said, "O.K., I'll pass it on."

It was so easy! Sally was feeling uplifted again, with
the sense of social achievement. Louise wasn't there.
They'd have a good time. The word was passed around,
and the gang went over to the Burnabys' where Jean
joined them, making toasted peanut-butter sandwiches
and chocolate milk. Scotty was more at ease with Jean

[57]

than at any time since last September.

Sally kept watching him, alert to every mood. Since Saturday evening, Scotty had become a very important person and she couldn't keep her attitude out of her face. She didn't want to be like that, but she couldn't help listening too alertly, watching him too closely, laughing too easily, making small possessive gestures.

"What's eating you, Sally?" he inquired once, in uneasy frankness.

"Why, nothing. What's wrong?"

"Oh, nothing, nothing, not a thing!" he said hastily. But the edge was off somewhere. Now what had she done?

Pinning up her hair that night, Sally felt let down. Sunday hadn't left her feeling as good as usual.

"Have a nice time?" she asked Jean, trying to be nonchalant. "I thought Jeff Sutton was kind of cute."

"Oh, he was all right," said Jean indifferently. "He's in one of my classes. I might go again. Does Hank Miller ever go?"

"Not so far," said Sally. "But you never can tell. Some of the others on the team have come one time or another. You know, I'm beginning to think Scotty is kind of special."

"Yeah," Jean was frank. "You sure put on an act for him tonight. Claws out and everything."

"Oh!" Sally hadn't thought it showed. "Well — if Louise can do it, I guess I can."

"I guess so," Jean yawned. "I don't know much about the facts of life, but I thought he looked a little nervous."

CURLED up in the big armchair next to the radio, Sally glowered at the game of solitaire spread out before her. This was the first Halloween she had spent at home since she was seven, and it was no fun.

Mother and dad were next door, spending the evening with the Careys. Jean was at Joyce's party; she was more congenial with that crowd since she had developed her crush on Hank Miller. Sally had refused an invitation to Becky's house because she knew Scotty and Louise would be there, and she couldn't face another evening like that one at Scotty's. So here she was sitting with Betsy and Jimmy, for lack of anything better to do.

Earlier in the evening they had gone out in costumes, demanding tricks or treats. Jimmy looked so important, and felt so big, to be going out after dark. They had come home with bags full of loot, and had gone to bed, exhausted, at eight. The excitement was over.

Sally looked up at the clock for the fourteenth time since eight thirty. Ten o'clock — time Ricky was getting in. He was out with his gang, with instructions to be home by ten.

The telephone rang sharply, and she jumped so that the game of solitaire was thrown into a heap. Drat those ghost stories! It was silly to listen to them, but when she did, they were too gripping to turn off. With her heart pounding heavily, she made her way across the empty room to the telephone.

" Hello? "

" Hello," she heard a very gruff voice at the other end. " Is this where Malcolm Burnaby lives? "

" Yes."

" Police headquarters. Your son is down here. Picked up for breaking street lights. You'll have to talk to us before we release him."

Sally clung to the receiver, trying desperately to think what to say. A memory of her mother's quick-thinking poise in emergencies flashed across her mind. With all the control she possessed, Sally tried to sound cool and poised.

" Thank you for calling, officer. Someone will come down to get him. But I don't know how soon we can get there."

" That's O.K., ma'am. It won't hurt him to wait in jail a bit."

Sally fumbled the receiver back on the hook and sank down on the nearest chair with shaking knees. She couldn't go: there was no one else in the house to be with Betsy and Jimmy. She'd have to call her parents. And mother had remarked how long it had been since they had spent an evening with the Careys.

Jail!

Ricky must be scared to death, poor kid. And he didn't mean anything — after all, it was Halloween. Unhappily she dialed the Carey number and asked to speak to her mother.

" Sally! What's wrong? "

" Nothing's wrong here, mother. The children are fine. But — Rick's in jail! "

"Oh, for goodness' sake!" She could just see the look on mother's face.

"They just called. He was breaking street lights, and you'll have to talk to the police before they let him go."

There was a moment's silence at the other end. Then mother's voice came through, calm as ever.

"We'll go right down, Sally. Don't worry about it."

Sally felt a little better as she watched for them at the window. In less than five minutes they came home to get the car. They didn't come into the house, but Sally could tell from the way dad walked out to the garage that he wasn't at all happy.

It was ten thirty, and there was no telling how long it would take to extricate Ricky. Sally made herself some cocoa and toast, wondering wistfully how Becky's party was going. Perhaps she had been hasty to refuse just because of Scotty. Only things were *so different* now. She finished her snack and wished Jean were home.

Eleven o'clock.

What if the police wouldn't release Rick?

Then the lights of the car flashed on the driveway. The garage door slid heavily shut, and her parents and Ricky came into the house, mother and dad looking very serious, Ricky white and scared. Dad motioned him to sit down on the straight desk chair, which he did, sideways, leaning his arms and chin on the back. Mother and dad sort of perched in a couple of armchairs as if they expected to jump up again. Sally huddled in the chair by the radio.

"You might as well understand, Richard," dad began, "that there is nothing funny about this business at all."

"No, sir," agreed Rick.

"Now, just exactly what happened?"

"Well, it was this way," Ricky began, eager to justify himself. "Mike and Slugger and Jeep and me, we were just walking along, kind of slow, not doing anything, and pretty soon Mike says to Slugger, 'Race you to that lamppost,' and Slugger lost and Mike says: 'O.K., you lose. You hafta throw a rock at the light.' So Slugger did, and then they raced to the next one, and —"

"Hold it," said his father peremptorily. "You're telling the wrong story. We want to know what *you* did!"

"That's what I'm coming to," said Rick patiently.

"Well, skip all the build-up!" instructed his father. "What did you do?"

"Well, it was this way," Ricky began again, with a hopeless look at Sally. She knew how he felt: you have to tell things from the beginning to get them straight.

"Begin with 'I,'" advised his father.

"O.K., O.K.," Rick conceded. "I lost a race to Slugger and I had to throw a rock at the light, and when I missed I had to keep on until I hit it, and on the second light the police came along."

His father's face relaxed slightly.

"Now we're getting somewhere," he said.

A key turned in the lock, the door opened on a chorus of gay farewells, and Jean came in from her party, sparkling and bright.

"It was a wonderful party!" she cried. Then she grasped the scene before her. "What's wrong?"

"Rick will tell you," said her mother. Jean dropped her coat on the chair by the door and sat down by Sally. Everyone waited for Rick. He looked at his shoes as he repeated the story.

"But after all, it's Halloween!" cried Jean. Ricky's face lighted up at this support.

[62]

Her father looked sterner than ever. " Let's get it all straight before we talk about it," he said.

" So then they took us to the station in the police car and kept us until our folks came. Mike and Slugger were still there when we came home."

Mr. Burnaby caught Mrs. Burnaby's eye and they seemed to agree about something.

" Did you think street lights cost less on Halloween perhaps? " dad asked.

" No," Rick mumbled, and Jean dropped her eyes. She was included in that question too.

" All right, then. Rick has made a mistake just as serious and expensive as it would be any day in the year. Now he seems to think it's all Mike and Slugger's fault."

" Well, they are terrible, dad! " cried Sally. " They're always taking bicycles and leaving them blocks away, and cheating in school, and swiping things at the dime stores — "

Her father looked enlightened.

" Then what was Ricky doing with them at all? " he inquired. " Didn't you know the kind of boys they are? "

Ricky nodded, reluctant and embarrassed.

" Yeah, but I see them around the Y — and on Halloween — after all — "

" After all, a police record on Halloween is just as bad as any other time," reminded his father. " I thought we had talked about bad company enough in this family so everyone knew how we felt about it. If you want to be a cheat and petty thief, just pick those boys for friends. If you want to be honest and straightforward, choose your friends accordingly."

Ricky nodded.

" But there is something more important than that, and this goes for all of you," he looked at the girls meaningly. " Nobody made Rick's mistake tonight but Ricky. He can't blame it on anyone else, no matter how he reasons about it. It took him a long time before he could get around to saying, ' I did this.' Forget the reasons, forget the other boys. *You* did this, and *you* have to make it good."

Ricky looked him straight in the face now.

" Yes, sir," he said.

" What are you going to do about it? "

Ricky was lacing his fingers in and out, sighing heavily. His father waited.

" Pay for the lights, I guess," Ricky muttered.

" You wouldn't expect someone else to pay for them, would you? "

" No," said Ricky, uncomfortably. " But — "

" It would be much less bother to forget the whole thing," agreed his father. " But unfortunately someone has to do it, and it looks as if you've elected yourself."

He grinned a little, and Ricky relaxed and grinned too.

" I'll give you some advice," his father offered, companionably. " When you're faced with a job like this, the more you duck it the harder it gets. Go out to meet it, and it will turn out to be a satisfaction to you. See what I mean? "

" I guess so," Ricky sounded baffled.

" All right, it's all up to you now. Just take a ride down to headquarters on your bike tomorrow and talk it over. They'll tell you how much it costs. There are lots of things around here that need doing — clean the basement, burn rubbish, take down screens — "

Ricky stood up with a certain pride.

" I guess I can find plenty of jobs," he said. " O.K., dad, I'll take care of the damage."

[64]

His father clapped him on the shoulder approvingly. "If you do, the damage won't be so important." He lighted a cigarette as the three children went up to bed.

Ricky came into the girls' room a minute, important with his responsibility.

"It was all kind of an accident," he said, with a note of apology. "How much do you suppose street lights cost, anyway?"

"I don't know," said Sally, setting out her bedroom slippers. "It shouldn't be terribly hard to earn the money."

Ricky was taking off his shoes and trying to make them hang on his ears. "I can earn it all right," he agreed. "Maybe I'll earn some extra, while I'm at it."

He went to his own room, looking quite cheered with the possibilities. Sally looked at Jean, hanging up her party dress.

"I'd rather be earning money myself than sitting around playing solitaire like tonight," she said. "With Christmas coming and everything — "

Jean looked out of the closet, startled. "My goodness!" she said. "Christmas already? And I've been spending all my money on clothes this month."

"Do you mind if I go ahead with the dinner dishes?" Sally asked her family a little impatiently a few days later. "Millie's coming over, and I've got to be through before eight!"

Dad raised his eyebrows at mother, as he usually did whenever Millie's name was mentioned.

"Again?" asked mother, in that quiet tone that implied controlled impatience. "It seems to me she's here a lot on school nights lately."

"Well —" Sally was already running water in the dishpan. She came back to the door. "She needs help with her Latin. Her folks want her to take College Boards and she really isn't very good. Besides, it helps my Latin to work with her."

"No doubt it's a great advantage to work with that featherbrain," said dad ironically. "Why doesn't Mrs. Davis help her, if she needs it so much?"

"Well, Mrs. Davis is so busy with all her organizations," Sally explained, "she's hardly ever home. And when she is, she's always telephoning."

"The complete and perfect explanation of why —" dad was beginning when mother interrupted. "After all, Malcolm, they are neighbors. Better not pass ideas around."

Sally went back to splash in the dishwater with exasperation. Mother still acted as if she were a child, refusing to discuss the neighbors. As if everyone didn't know the reason Millie was the way she was. Sally felt, virtuously, that if she could influence Millie for the better she had an obligation to do so. Someday the family would understand.

The doorbell rang just as she finished, and she rinsed the suds off her hands and grabbed a towel. She could hear Millie graciously greeting her parents.

"We'll go up to my room," she said quickly, as she turned off the kitchen light. "Can you study down here all right, Jean?"

"Oh, sure," Jean agreed, "but don't be too late, will you?"

Sally settled her guest at the double desk in her bedroom, and Millie opened her books with a sigh.

"I don't know why I waste my time on this stuff," she brooded. "The folks think I'm going to college. But not

[66]

if I can help it."

"What else would you do?" Sally had never thought of anything after high school except college.

Millie shrugged discontentedly and leaned her elbows on the desk. "What I really want to do is get married."

"Married! But — I mean, already?"

Millie nodded until her silver-blond hair fell around her face.

"You bet! After all, I'm eighteen. I don't want a job, and I hate to study. Anyway — you don't know what our house is like. The sooner I can have a place of my own, the better."

Sally was shocked. But underneath Millie's bitter words she could sense the girl's aching frustration.

"But you have a lovely house, Millie. Such pretty furniture and wallpaper. Ours is kind of shabby, it seems to me."

"But yours is a home," said Millie enviously. "Your folks are here, mostly. And your dad sits around at night and acts as if he liked his family. Mother is never home — *never!* She belongs to about fifteen clubs and goes to twelve board meetings, and in between she's so busy talking to all the officers and investigating conditions that — oh, well, that's how it is. We never have any fun together."

There was nothing Sally could say. She looked at Millie with more sympathy than she had ever felt for the girl.

"Oh, well," said Millie, turning back to the Latin text with a philosophic wave of the hand, "anyway, if I were married, I'd have someone to have fun with and talk to — and I'd like to have my own family. Believe me, it would be different from the one I've got now!"

For five minutes they worked on Latin. Then Millie

[67]

raised her head with a light giggle.

"You'll never guess who's dating me tomorrow night!"

"Tomorrow!" Sally forgot the Latin immediately. "Do you go out on school nights?"

"Why, of course!" said Millie. "Don't you?"

Sally was embarrassed. It sounded so juvenile not to.

"Why, not much," she said hesitantly. "Mother and dad said no dates on school nights right from the beginning. So I never have."

Millie raised delicate eyebrows.

"My folks let me decide for myself," she said blandly. "Anyway, I'm going out with Rodney Miller." She paused impressively.

"O Millie! You mean that cute boy in your history class?"

Millie nodded. "Honestly, he's too cute! I'll bet you we're going steady by Christmas!"

Sally kept thinking of Millie's plan for her future. "But you wouldn't marry any of these boys, would you?"

Millie laughed. "They're too young. But it's good practice. One of these days I'll meet someone a little older. You wait and see."

Looking at Millie, with the lamplight shining on her silvery hair, and the dark lashes shadowing her blue eyes, Sally wondered how anyone could resist her. But the conversation left her with a peculiar feeling.

"Sally! Are you watching the time?" mother reminded her from downstairs.

It was maddening to have someone always know what you were doing, but in a way it was comforting too. You weren't quite so free to make mistakes as Millie was, for instance. They plunged into the Latin again, and Sally had almost finished the passage when Millie remembered another secret of vital importance. She didn't know, simply couldn't imagine, what Vic was going to say about Rodney.

"Why should he care?" asked Sally, as she was expected to do.

"You should know Vic! He's just furious when I speak to another boy in the hall! He'll be fit for murder, that's all, if he finds out about this date!"

It all sounded very exciting and a little strange. But it was after nine and the Latin was far from finished. Sally managed to complete her own translation and dragged Millie through five lines, when Millie had to tell her of the violent quarrel she'd had with Vic last week. Honestly, she'd thought he was never going to speak to her again. But — could you believe it! — he called the very next night.

Suddenly it was ten o'clock, and Mrs. Burnaby knocked on the door and looked in with a grave face. "Ten o'clock, girls," she said.

Sally felt hot and chagrined. But Millie looked up with a charming smile.

"I'll have to be going," she said. "I do appreciate your help, Sally!"

She gathered up her books, made her farewells, and went home. Mrs. Burnaby sat down at the desk.

"Sally, I've never said much about your friends. But I really think Millie is not quite — you don't have much in common, do you?"

"Well, now that Kate isn't going to high school, Millie and I just seem to have to go together — being on the same block and everything. And it's kind of hard not to see her on the side, then."

"I know," mother nodded, as if she really did. "And,

of course, they are neighbors. But I'd hate to have you be like her."

" Oh, heavens! " Sally dismissed the possibility with a horrified face. " But she does have some good points. She's very friendly and she's certainly nice to you."

" Oh, she knows her manners," agreed Mrs. Burnaby, " but I'm afraid she has two sets: one for her crowd, and one for grownups, and that's a bad sign. Just don't encourage her to come over on school nights if you can manage. Here it is ten o'clock, and you've just barely finished your Latin."

Sally blushed at the truth of the statement. It was embarrassing to think that mother might have heard Millie's conversation, but she was afraid she had. Mother patted her on the shoulder, smiled for the first time that evening, and left her to finish her work. Jean came in, curled up with a book, and read until Sally began to undress. Then she propped herself on her elbow to watch the preparations for retiring. She had some confidences of her own to make.

" Did you hear about Hank Miller? " she demanded.

" No, what about him? "

" He may be homely," said Jean in a dreamy tone, " but he's got so much more than looks! And when you remember that wonderful pass he caught just last Saturday and ran down the field and saved the game — well, anyway, he's simply too marvelous."

" Uh-huh." Sally had heard most of this before.

" Anyway, today I was hurrying out of English class, talking to Jeff — you remember, he goes to St. Paul's — Well, I was talking to Jeff, and Hank came swinging around the corner, the way he does, and knocked my books right on the floor! " She paused in happy reminiscence.

"Kind of clumsy, I'd say," remarked Sally absently.

"Yes, but *cute!*" Jean insisted. "Anyway, then he picked them all up, and said, 'Gee, excuse me!' in the most *apologetic* voice, and smiled!"

Sally smiled ruefully. She could remember her freshman crushes, and how comfortably remote the whole business was! Nothing like the complications she faced in her senior year.

"It's kind of nice," she said. "Now, me — all I have to think about is how mad Scotty makes me these days."

"I should think!" Jean knew all about Scotty's defection, but only from Sally. He himself was as friendly as ever when he went past the house. But he always went past, now.

"It isn't as if I was crazy about him, or anything. It's his attitude! It's the principle of the thing. Besides, I never went out with anyone else much, and now how can I go to the dances?"

"It's maddening," agreed Jean, who had never had to cope with a similar problem. "But why not look around for someone else and surprise him?"

"Well, who else is there?" Sally dismissed the rest of the senior class scornfully. "I never did like most of them much. But, on the other hand, I suppose it wouldn't hurt to be nice to the boys in my classes. I'd hate to miss the football dance — and the winter formal — and this is my year for the Senior Ball! I was so used to Scotty, and he was so handy! Seems to me all I do now is sit around."

"Speaking of sitting," said Jean slowly, "lots of girls do it. For money, I mean."

"Speaking of money," Sally returned, "I wish I had more. Christmas is coming, and I saw a wonderful new sweater set the other day, and my stadium boots are practically worn out. I don't know where all the money goes."

"And I still need more clothes," Jean brooded.

"Why don't we be sitters?" Both girls said the words at the same time and burst into giggles. Mother knocked on the door.

"Girls!" she said severely. "For goodness' sake, get to bed, *now*! Look at the time!"

She switched out the light with an emphatic snap that meant it was to stay out. Sally crept noiselessly into the bathroom to brush her teeth. But, back in bed, she had one more whispered word with Jean: "I think we've got something! Let's work on it tomorrow!"

THE sitting plan was announced with appropriate solemnity at dinner the following evening. Mother and dad listened attentively.

"I don't know, girls," said mother. "It really takes more time than you think."

"Time is what I've got plenty of," Sally pointed out.

"And the girls say everyone is desperate for sitters," added Jean. "It would be a public service."

"Jeepers!" exclaimed Ricky, feeling like a man of distinction, since he was paying for the street lights. "Lookit all the money you'll earn! I wish boys could be sitters. Of all the soft jobs!"

"Soft!" exclaimed Sally, outraged. "If you had ever tried to take care of other people's children for all afternoon, while they're crying for their mothers and whining and fussing with each other, you wouldn't call it soft!"

"How do you know it'll be like that?" asked mother, interestedly. "You haven't tried it yet."

"Oh, the other girls tell me about it," said Sally vaguely.

"Why do you choose such a drastic way of earning a living?" inquired her father.

Sally shrugged. "Oh, it might not be quite as bad as they say," she admitted. "And at least I can do it eve-

nings, when there's nothing else to do. When the kids
are in bed, I can get a lot of studying done."

Ricky intercepted the wink her father gave her
mother.

"Just what I said," he announced, triumphantly.
"Easy!"

"It does take patience," said her mother, warningly,
"and a keen sense of responsibility. I don't know that
I'm entirely in favor — "

"O mother!" Sally interrupted with exaggerated patience. "You know it won't be dangerous! For heaven's
sake! And besides, you're right here, if anything too terrible happened."

"I think it was Samuel Johnson who said that a man
is seldom more innocently employed than when he is
earning money," said her father. "It'll probably be a
good experience for both of you — learning that people
pay you only for doing what they want you to do. Only
don't get the idea that the money is the most important
thing. It's convenient, but it is secondary."

Ricky had been attentively cleaning up the scraps in
the serving dishes. He burst into the conversation with
an idea of his own.

"Say, I guess I wouldn't mind having some of this
money that's floating around! How would it be if I got
a paper route, or something, dad? Can I? Maybe I
could buy that dog for myself. Or a car, or something."

"A car!" his mother stared in amazement.

"Well, lookit the swell jalopy Scotty got last spring.
He worked five years for that. Maybe I better start!"

"Mother, could I — if I raked the lawn, would you
give me a dime?" asked Betsy.

"I could rake the lawn," Jimmy announced. "I'd do
it for a nickel."

[74]

Dad leaned a weary head on one hand and waved the other for quiet.

"Now hold it! One at a time. Sally and Jean can try this sitting, if they are sure they can keep it under control. And don't get too tired. Or give up important things at school."

He drew a deep breath and looked at his elder son. "I don't know whether you could keep a job or not, Rick," he deliberated.

"Aw, gee whiz!" expostulated Rick. "Lots of smaller guys than me do it. Lookit Bucky Johnson!"

"Well," said his father, "it's up to you. If you can go to the news agency and get the job, and be on time and keep it — more power to you. But don't expect me to carry the papers two or three nights a week. And evenings only. No getting up at four o'clock in the dark."

"I think we're safe there," said mother. Ricky was already calculating how fast his fortune would pile up.

"I'll do the lawn too," he said largely, "but it'll cost you half a buck."

"I said I'd do the lawn," screamed Betsy. "Dibs! I said it first!"

Mother raised a quieting hand again. "Relax," she advised Betsy, who was quivering with excitement. "Ten cents an hour for the lawn. Betsy takes it first; and if she can't finish, Ricky can take over. Jimmy can help," she smiled at the youngest Burnaby, who was listening attentively to the program.

"I'll finish it over the week end as usual," said father pessimistically.

"There won't be any left." Betsy was all smiles again, and she tossed her braids triumphantly back and glared at Ricky.

"I'll call Mrs. Dale," Sally was planning with Jean.

"You tell Mrs. Clark. Those cute twins ought to be fun."
The Clarks lived on the corner, two doors away.

Jean looked into the future with starry eyes. "The Clark baby ought to be here by Christmas. Suppose we could help take care of it?"

"Maybe by next summer," said mother, not too hopefully. "Newborns are something else again. But you can try sitting for a while. You can always give it up."

Jean and Sally compared notes after the telephone calls. Both mothers were delighted to find someone in the block to help with their children, and promised to tell their friends.

"Mrs. Clark wants me for Saturday afternoon," said Jean, with mixed pleasure. "She wants to go to the university game with Mr. Clark. I don't see how I can miss the high-school game, but it's the first job. What on earth shall I tell her? I had to say I'd call her back."

Sally thought it over. "I'll take it," she offered. "You go ahead to the game. I don't mind missing it so much."

"Don't you really?" asked Jean. "I didn't want to turn her down, but when I thought of missing one of Hank's games — and there's only about one more — I just didn't see how I could."

"That's where it's going to be so handy, both of us doing it," said Sally. "I'll take this one. Sometime you can take a call for me."

The game really didn't matter much these days. She couldn't help thinking about Scotty, and it was all too evident that he never thought of her. Better to fill the time with a worth-while activity and try to forget.

All the same, it did seem peculiar to be sitting with Carolyn and Catherine Clark, the three-year-old twins, on a Saturday afternoon. Thinking of the other girls munching popcorn and singing the school songs and yelling for the touchdowns, Sally wasn't entirely sure she'd want to miss another game.

She found herself a little uneasy as the senior Clarks drove off. The girls were in bed, and she had full instructions for the afternoon: " Take them to the bathroom first thing, when they wake up. Then dress them — they need help with that. And give them a glass of milk and a graham cracker and take them outdoors. They'd better wear snow suits this afternoon." Easy enough.

Sally waited impatiently for the twins to wake up, wondering what was happening at the game. Would Jean go to the Ranch House? Wouldn't Kate be surprised to hear about her sitting?

Thinking of Kate suddenly reminded her of the college application that should have gone in a week ago. Their senior adviser had warned them in September not to delay in filling out entrance applications, and here it was November! She'd have to get busy with it as soon as she got home. Only she had wanted to talk it over first with Kate, who *thought* she was going to Conover, in Wisconsin. What if she had changed her mind?

" Mommy! " twin wails brought her back to the job on hand. She dashed up to the girls' room where Carolyn and Catherine were sitting up in their cribs, looking at her with the utmost suspicion.

" Come on, darlings," said Sally brightly, picking up the first one she came to. The little girl stiffened in her arms and screamed like a steam whistle. The other one buried her head in the bedclothes and howled dismally. Sally's heart sank.

" Want milk and graham cracker? " she offered. " Go outdoors? "

It was no good. They wanted mommy or nothing.

[77]

What on earth did you do now? She couldn't just let them scream until their parents came home. Sally set the little girl down on the rug — where she promptly threw herself headlong, still screaming — and tackled the other one.

That was no good either. This twin was as un-co-operative as her sister. They didn't want to go to the bathroom, they refused to have shoes put on, they wouldn't look at their dresses.

So this was baby sitting! No wonder the girls referred to it as " bratting " and sighed with implied martyrdom whenever they had a job.

Trying to think of something to do, Sally wandered about the room, looking at the pink-and-white checked gingham curtains and ruffles, the little white armchair with a pink-checked cushion, and the tiny matching rocker. It was a sweet room. Too bad the twins weren't as cute as their furniture. She looked sourly at them over her shoulder and picked up a few blocks, little red and blue and yellow cubes, with animals cut in relief on the sides. Idly she built them into a tower, growing interested herself as she piled up ten. Would the pile take another? It would. With the next one it began to teeter. Then it fell, scattering blocks all over the white shag rug.

Sally hadn't played with blocks since she'd been in kindergarten, but it was still fun to see how high the pile could grow without toppling. She began another stack. Just as it started to teeter, she realized that the screaming had stopped. Stealing a glance over her shoulder she found the twins watching her with sulky curiosity. Some instinct told her to keep on. She piled the blocks with greatest care, rising to her feet to reach the top of a really creative piece of engineering.

[78]

The twins were coming closer now. Curiosity had got the better of them, and they were as excited as Sally at the height the tower was achieving. One more block made it almost as high as her shoulder. Then it fell.

With squeals of delight, the twins scrambled to pick up the blocks.

"Do it again!" they begged, throwing blocks at her feet. Sally did it again. And again. The twins were captivated, and Sally felt the heady sensation of success.

Then an expression of dismay crossed one twin's face, and she looked down at the rug. Sally looked too. They had forgotten about the bathroom!

Horror-stricken, Sally sprang up and grabbed the wet twin and rushed her out of the room. She should have thought of the other one, and when she did it was already too late. What would Mrs. Clark say? That lovely white rug!

Sally felt like an utter failure. Beside this calamity the fact that the twins had stopped howling seemed of no significance. She mopped up with a bath towel and found fresh panties for the girls. Mrs. Clark would surely never have her back again.

Sitting in twin high chairs, down in the kitchen, the girls bubbled in their milk, dipped their graham crackers in their cups, until the crackers crumbled all over the trays and the floor, and began giggling together as each thought of new ways to play with the food. Sally was baffled. Surely children weren't like this all the time! They were so messy and independent. They didn't respond to her cautious suggestions. Something told her that their mother would never allow such messy eating. But how could she stop them?

Mentally Sally was wringing her hands, while outwardly she tried to be calm. After two glasses of milk apiece and four double graham crackers had been spilled and crushed, she decided it would be safe to say "no more." To her surprise the children agreed without a murmur. Moistening a towel, she washed faces and hands and trays. The little girls watched her, and she suspected that they were plotting some subtle new horror. Then she decided to chance their screams. She let them sit where they were while she wiped up the floor and washed the glasses.

The twins watched her without protest, and the job was done in a few minutes. Sally's sense of achievement revived. Now for snow suits. Lifting them down, she asked them where the wraps were. To her surprise, one twin immediately started for the coat closet and began tugging at a powder-blue snow suit with a red lining. A red one with powder-blue lining was hanging next to it.

"What's your name?" Sally asked as she inserted small feet into the suit and pulled it up over the child's shoulders.

"Carolyn," said the child, immediately overcome with giggles. That was something, Sally thought. Now she knew which one was which. Carolyn in the blue suit, Catherine in the red.

By now they treated her like an old friend. Outdoors, they invited her to rake leaves, play ball, get out their tricycles.

"Why, this is fun!" Sally suddenly realized, as she threw the ball to Catherine, who caught it in both chubby arms and squealed with delight. Carolyn energetically raked leaves until it was her turn to play ball. Teaching them to catch the ball was an absorbing business. They tried so hard, and their co-ordination was so unsteady. Sally was as thrilled as they were, each time they caught it. The three of them were still playing when the Clarks arrived. Sally had had no idea the time was passing so fast.

"Hello, darlings!" cried Mrs. Clark, climbing out of the car and coming across the lawn. "This is just wonderful!" she exclaimed to Sally, with vivacious enthusiasm. "None of our sitters has got out and played with them before! I know they loved it!"

Sally remembered the early failure.

"I'm terribly sorry, Mrs. Clark," she said, blushing hotly, "but they were kind of — unhappy, when they woke up — and we all forgot about the bathroom — and I'm afraid they spoiled the rug in their room!"

Mrs. Clark laughed gaily.

"That's happened before," she said. "Don't give it a thought! They look happy, and that's the main thing.

I'd love to have you come again! "

She gave her a dollar for the four hours, and Sally went home feeling rich and successful. It had been an easy way, after all, to earn twenty-five cents an hour. The twins were adorable. She felt as if she could cope with children any time, now.

" How did you get along? " asked mother, as soon as she came into the house. Sally was bubbling inside with the warm feeling of accomplishment. This was something she had thought of and done all by herself and it had worked.

" It was O.K.," she said.

" Mrs. Dale called," reported her mother. " She wants you for Wednesday before Thanksgiving."

" That's wonderful! " said Sally, going to the telephone with a springing step.

CHAPTER
EIGHT

>>

"NEXT Saturday night?" Sally leafed through her
engagement book. "Why, yes, I think so. At eight.
I'll be glad to come, Mrs. Dale."

The sitting program was a huge success, naturally.
The mothers of small children in the neighborhood always had difficulty finding sitters, and the Burnaby
girls were responsible and obliging. Sally's time was
filled faster than she had hoped.

At first she hesitated a little about Saturday nights.
But after another disappointing evening at Becky's, and
two Saturday nights of staying home without even a
date for the movies, why not oblige the neighbors and
earn some money?

Her mother looked up from a pile of socks that had
accumulated for mending.

"I hate to see you tie up all your nights with business
and never have fun any more."

"I wouldn't mind having fun," said Sally with bitter
frankness, "but there doesn't seem to be any coming
my way. Most of the boys are going steady, and they
thought Scotty and I were, and there we are. I might
as well forget about fun in my senior year."

Mother looked surprised and disturbed, as if she
thought times had changed since she was young.

"Surely everyone in the school isn't going steady!"
she said.

"Well, most of them," said Sally. "Anyway — "

"Anyway, with Kate gone, there's no one to tell you what to do," said her mother shrewdly. "Don't you think it's time you began to figure things out for yourself?"

Sally flushed. She was over the first painful adjustment of life, without her best friend and without her dependable date. But it was still simpler to drift along than to take the initiative.

"You wouldn't want me to chase the boys the way Millie does," she defended herself.

"Certainly not!" Mother snipped the thread from the finished darn. "But all your life you will have to make some effort to be agreeable and make friends — boys and girls alike. You need both kinds, and you can't expect them to do all the work."

"Well — " Sally was uncertain how much she wanted to do.

"There's no reason why you shouldn't be friendly with the boys in your classes. You don't have to be pushing or suggestive or coy. Just let them know you think they're nice people and they will think the same of you. You'd better learn to make the effort now, when you need to, or you may have a dull time in college. It's never smart to depend on one person all the time."

Sally considered her mother's words without seeming to. She certainly wouldn't look forward to college if it was going to be like this.

"Speaking of college," her mother looked up again, "have you sent out your applications yet?"

Sally shook her head. "Not yet," she said listlessly. "I just can't seem to make up my mind. When Kate comes home at Christmas, maybe we can decide something."

"When Kate comes home," said her mother tartly, "it may be too late. You know how hard it is to get into schools these days — and how early you should look around."

Sally shrugged impatiently. If mother just wouldn't worry about her life so! "I'll figure something out," she said shortly. "That's all I hear at school — 'What do you want to do with your life?' How should I know?"

"No one can figure it out for you," observed her mother, ignoring her daughter's impatience. "Part of growing up is taking responsibility and meeting deadlines. You can't let everything go until you're good and ready."

Sally rose abruptly. She couldn't stand any more of this tiresome talk about the future. As if the present weren't enough of a problem! "I'll think about it," she said sulkily, as she went up to bed.

She did think about it, long enough to scribble a note to Kate. Corresponding, even with Kate, was the hardest thing Sally had to do. But this college question had to be settled soon. She found her stationery and began to write rapidly.

There! Licking the envelope, Sally felt practically as if she had been accepted for college. Kate was probably still going to Conover, but she ought to know definitely before she made final plans herself. Sighing with satisfaction, she climbed into bed and went to sleep.

With the end of the football season, basketball began. This year Jean needed no urging to go to the games. She ruthlessly turned down sitting engagements for any afternoon or evening when one was scheduled. And before the third game she had a crush on a center.

Sally hardly knew her sister. Jean, who only last summer thought boys were silly, who cared nothing for her appearance when school began, was curling her hair every night and worrying constantly about what to wear to school — it must be a different outfit every day. The sitting money augmented her dress allowance, but still there was hardly enough.

Sally herself was taking her mother's words to heart. It made sense to be friendly with the people in your classes, and it was easier, now that she was beginning to feel so efficient. And it was easier too, with her sitting successes on her mind, to forget about Scotty.

Al Carter, the basketball center, was in Sally's history class, and, inspired by Jean's enthusiasm, she made up her mind to let him know she thought he was nice. He was tall and thin and shy with the girls. One day, when Sally found they were going out of the door together, she smiled up at him and said, "I thought your question about the economic forces in the ratification of the Constitution was very good, and Mr. Whaley seemed to think so too."

"Gee, did you?" Al seemed gratified.

After that it was easy to smile at him and toss him a cheerful hello, as if she had known him a long time. She wasn't going to have the whirlwind kind of conquest that Millie boasted of, but at least she could be friendly with someone outside of the small group she was used to.

Jean was bubbling with excitement when she found that Sally was on speaking terms with her new hero.

"Al Carter is simply divine! He's so cute — tall and kind of gangly, with that sort of shy smile as if he wasn't any good at all, when everybody knows he simply won the game! I don't know how he could help being conceited when everybody — but everybody — is mad about him."

That, Sally considered, was mild exaggeration. Most of the girls conceded that Al could play basketball, but beyond that he was pretty dim.

"What about Hank?" Ricky teased her at the dinner table. Jean's crush had gone beyond privacy. The whole family knew about it, and she didn't care at all.

"Oh — Hank! Well, I guess he can play football all right. But I think he's very conceited. You can just tell the way he walks down the hall, as if everybody was watching! And Joyce told me Pete told her he never reads a book. He just gets by because the team needed him. I can't stand him any more!"

"Al Carter is better than that," Sally informed her. "He gave a good answer today." Jean glowed immediately. "What's he really like? Isn't he pretty brilliant?"

"Well, kind of. It's hard to tell, because he's so quiet. He doesn't recite much. But he generally knows the answers when he's called on."

"Of course," Jean was satisfied. "That tall, quiet type is apt to be very deep, I think."

Dad took a long drink of milk and winked at Betsy.

"How's Superman, Bets? Pretty brilliant these days?"

"Oh, sure!" Betsy tossed her braids back over her shoulders. "He's way ahead of these earthbound creatures."

"Well, Al Carter's O.K.," Ricky defended his sister's hero. "You gotta stay with the earthbound creatures when you're in a basketball game. Superman would be ineligible."

Jean twinkled happily at her father, who grinned at

all of them. The telephone rang and Sally jumped up.

"Hello?"

"Sally?" An unfamiliar masculine voice came over the line.

"Yes. Who is this? Oh! Al Carter! Why, how are you?"

"Why, I wondered — that is, I thought, I mean, do you have — will you go to the football dance with me?"

Sally nearly dropped the telephone. A date! And for the first big dance of the year. "I'd love to, Al. It will be loads of fun. I'll be seeing you."

"Well, for heaven's sake!" She almost fell into her place at the table with the excitement of her news. "Guess what!"

"What?" Ricky promptly asked.

"That was a date for the football dance — and it's Al Carter!"

Jean's mouth dropped open, and she looked from Sally to her mother to her father and back to Sally. "For goodness' sake!" she whispered. "Al Carter! Oh, my!"

It was mother who remembered about that Wednesday. "Haven't you promised Mrs. Dale you'd sit that night?"

"Oh, yes!" Sally had felt she was forgetting something about that particular date. "Well, I'll just cancel. There's over a week to get someone else."

Dad looked concerned. "If she can, Sally. You can't disappoint someone, you know —"

"Oh, I can fix it some way," Sally assured him airily.

"That means he'll be coming here," Jean murmured half to herself. "Al Carter in this house. I'll see him — and meet him — Sally, isn't it simply wonderful? Aren't you too excited to breathe?"

"Not quite," Sally assured her, "but it will be fun." The most fun, she thought to herself, was going to be showing Scotty that she could go to a dance without him.

There was no time to call Mrs. Dale that night, because she was going somewhere else to sit at seven thirty. Mother was rather dubious about sitting on school nights. The girls assured her that they could always study, and did. But mother pointed out that they were frequently very late getting home.

The next night Sally remembered Mrs. Dale at nine o'clock, and just as she moved toward the telephone, it rang. She picked it up and another unfamiliar masculine voice asked for Jean.

Sally called her sister with a tingle of excitement. As far as anyone knew, this was the first call Jean had ever had from a boy. Jean came away from the telephone with calm nonchalance and went back to her books.

"Who was it?" Sally couldn't bear not to know.

"That was Jeff — that boy in my class, you know. He goes to St. Paul's too. Kind of homely with glasses. He wants me to go to the football dance."

Well! Jean's first date, and she acted as if she didn't even care. Sally was the one who was excited. "Jean! We can trade a dance!"

"Sally!" Now the dance was important. Sally remembered Mrs. Dale again.

"I'd better call Mrs. Dale right away," she said, dialing the number. Perhaps she'd been a little hasty to fill her book with sitting engagements so fast. "Mrs. Dale? This is Sally Burnaby. Something has come up for me for the Wednesday before Thanksgiving. Do you suppose you could get someone else?" Mrs. Dale sounded vaguely annoyed, and Sally remembered her father's words. "If you can't, of course I'll come. Just let me know." Of course Mrs. Dale wouldn't have any trouble. She knew lots of sitters.

Jean was in the closet, going through her clothes. "I'll simply have to get a dress," she announced, poking her head out. "My goodness, I never expected to go to a party like this! I haven't a thing to wear."

"I'll go with you," offered Sally. Never in her life had she gone out to choose a dress without help, usually Kate's. Jean accepted her offer graciously, but without enthusiasm. Actually, Sally realized, Jean would feel perfectly competent to pick out a dress by herself. Sally had to admire her self-reliance.

As it turned out, Jean was glad to have Sally along on Saturday. Mother gave Jean her December allowance in advance, with the warning that there wouldn't be any more until after New Year's. And when Jean faced the rack of date dresses, she was uncertain what to choose after all.

Sally loved to look at clothes. Expertly she passed dress after dress along the rack, rejecting them.

"Not that red," she said, "too bright. A soft crimson, maybe — not that gaudy green, either. And this one is terrible — limp and dowdy. Here's one that might be good."

They selected three dresses to try on, and Jean's choice was the winner after all: midnight-blue velveteen, with cap sleeves and a dirndl skirt and a narrow gold-kid belt.

"It's perfect on you," said Sally, as Jean stared, dazzled at the glamorous reflection in the glass.

"But what about shoes?" Jean wailed, looking at her feet. "This dress takes all of my allowance, and my Sunday pumps won't look right at all!"

While the clerk wrapped the dress, they calculated possible earnings from their sitting jobs, and decided that mother wouldn't mind too much if they charged some suede sandals and sheer nylon hose.

"This is over the budget," Jean demurred, "but I'll earn the money and give it to mother before the bill comes in."

Mother looked a little unsettled about the shoes. But she conceded that if Jean earned the money to pay for them, it would be all right this time.

"You'll have to plan better next time," she warned them both. "It's poor business to earn the money after you buy the things, and extra charges can be very awkward for us."

Then the blow fell. Mrs. Dale called on Monday night to say that she'd been trying since the week before to get someone to replace Sally, and everyone was busy that night.

"I wouldn't care," she said over the phone, trying to be conciliatory, "only we've got theater tickets, and it's an anniversary, and I don't see how we can change our plans. If we'd known a week or two earlier — "

This was a crisis. Sally hung up the telephone and turned to Jean, aghast.

"I don't know how I can get out of it," she said unhappily. "Dad wouldn't let me disappoint her, and I suppose it is my own responsibility."

"But you promised Al Carter," cried Jean, more upset than her sister. "You can't do that to him! I'd stay home myself — only — "

"That wouldn't get you anywhere," said Sally gloomily. "You couldn't even meet him, if you were off sitting somewhere. And you can't disappoint Jeff."

The situation looked black. Sally sighed heavily. The

only thing to do now was to talk to mother about it. Together she and Jean went down to the living room,
where mother and dad were listening to John Jacob
Niles singing old ballads.

"That melody derives from fourteenth-century English folk song," dad was explaining, as the girls entered.
They waited until the record was finished.

"Mother!" Sally began, as the record stopped. "The
most awful thing has happened!"

Mother looked up and dad obligingly stopped the
machine. "Is Kate coming back?" asked dad. Sally
ignored his effort at wit.

"Mrs. Dale can't get anyone else for Wednesday
night!"

"Sally simply can't cancel Al Carter," said Jean, im-
ploringly.

"Jean can't stay home from her first dance — when
she's got her dress and everything," said Sally helplessly. "It's an awful mess. I wish we'd never started
sitting!"

"I was afraid of something like this," said mother, as
if she was thinking hard. "It's too bad, and of course
you can't disappoint Mrs. Dale."

Sally turned to Jean. "You see?"

Jean drew a quivering breath. "I don't want to go at
all, if Sally doesn't go."

"Well —" mother looked at dad. "I don't know what
you can do. It seems to me it's your problem."

The girls looked at each other.

"O.K., then. Maybe we'll both cancel our dates."

"Don't do anything tonight," mother advised. "Go
upstairs and think it over. Tomorrow is soon enough to
talk to the boys."

Drooping, the girls climbed the stairs again.

[92]

"I hate to disappoint Jeff," said Jean, staring at the blue dress in the closet.

Sally chewed on her pencil. She hated to give up her hopes of surprising Scotty.

"I'll try the girls I know," she said pessimistically.

She spent an hour on the telephone. Of the five girls she knew who did sitting, three were going to the football dance, and the other two were already engaged to sit that night.

"Let me try," said Jean, reaching for the telephone. "I know a couple of others."

They were busy too. Sally thumbed her engagement book dolefully.

"It'll probably happen again," she mused. "Maybe we should figure out some way not to get tied up like this."

Jean looked at the book over her shoulder.

"I'm not going to give any night over a week ahead," she said firmly. "That would help. But I can't stop sitting for a while. I owe mother seven-fifty for those shoes. The more money we have, the more we need, seems as if."

Sally frowned thoughtfully. "Maybe that's what dad meant when he said to keep it under control," she said, understanding his warning for the first time. "You'd better go to the dance, Jean. I'll go to Mrs. Dale's. There's no sense in both of us missing the dance." She sighed heavily with renunciation, just as mother knocked lightly and came into the room.

"What's the situation?" she asked cheerfully.

"There isn't anyone else," Sally reported gloomily. "We've tried everyone we know. I'll just have to tell Al I can't go."

Mother looked from one serious face to the other.

"I've been thinking it over," she said, sitting down on Sally's bed. "I think it's pretty important for Sally to keep her date. So I will sit with the Dales that night."

"Mother!" Sally cried joyfully. Then she said apologetically, "I hate to have you do it, though."

"It's not because I enjoy sitting," said her mother with a frank grimace. "Just try to arrange things a little better another time. Don't fill all your time so far ahead. You need the social life too."

"It'll be a pleasure!" Sally assured her mother, with an appreciative hug.

>>>

CHAPTER NINE

MILLIE telephoned a couple of days before the
football dance to tell Sally she was going with
Eddie Lansing, who was terribly smooth. She had met
another boy, but he was older and she couldn't get him
interested in high-school dances. But she kind of
thought he was The One.

She chattered on and on while Sally's thoughts trav-
eled a road of their own. Mother was probably right
about Millie, but, on the other hand, the girl *was* lonely.
Anyone could tell from her conversation. Almost without intending to, Sally said, " I'll be seeing you at the
football dance."

" Oh! " Millie sounded startled and then pleased.
" Really? Who's your date? "

" Al Carter." Sally wished she hadn't brought it up
after all.

" Look," Millie was exclaiming at the other end of
the wire, " why don't we make it a double date? You
ought to meet Eddie. And we could trade dances — "

" Cut it short," dad called from the other room. " It's
been twenty-five minutes now! For the love of Pete! "

" I've got to go," Sally said hurriedly into the phone.
" I don't think I can double with you, Millie. Jean has
a date for it too. We'll see you there." She hung up

with a mixed-up feeling of annoyance at having her calls regulated by her father, and relief at getting away from Millie.

She was surprised at how eagerly she looked forward to this date with Al Carter, and she tried to repress her enthusiasm superstitiously. Try not to expect anything, she had decided, weeks ago. The less you expect, the less you will be disappointed.

Jean had no such qualms. She was ecstatic about meeting Al Carter, actually dancing with him. He was much more important than Jeff.

Dinner was sketchy the night of the dance. Sally refused to eat much, for fear it would make her tummy too fat for her dress, and Jean couldn't eat from excitement. No one was interested in doing dishes, but dad recruited Ricky and told mother and the girls to run along: they'd surprise them all.

Up in the green-striped bedroom, Sally and Jean were engrossed with the final steps in the ritual of dressing. Jean watched Sally work on her eyebrows, but declined to fuss with her own. However, she took great pains to put on exactly the right amount of lipstick.

The bell rang at quarter past eight, just as they were ready to step into their dresses. Jean's eyes flew to meet Sally's. Who would it be? They stood frozen a minute, listening.

"How do you do?" Dad answered the door.

"How do you do, Mr. Burnaby," they heard a nervous voice say. "I'm Jeffrey Sutton, Jean's date."

"Come in, Jeff, come right in! I was just playing some records you might like." Dad was changing the record as he talked. "Like folk music? Some of these cowboy things are pretty good."

"Yes, sir, that's good, all right," Jeff said.

Jean's dress was fastened. She took a last look at herself, and suddenly her self-confidence wilted.

"Do I look all right?" she asked in a whisper. "Should I go down now?"

"Yes," Sally looked her over once more. "Go ahead. You look lovely. We'll see you at the dance."

Jean floated away, and Sally tiptoed out into the hall to listen. Rick let out a long whistle as she came down the stairs, and Sally winced. He ought to be shut up, honestly!

"Well, well, well," said dad heartily, and Sally winced again. Why did fathers have to be like that?

"It certainly makes me feel old to have *two* girls stepping out!" Dad was going on, a little louder than normal: "Be a good girl, Jeanie. Don't stay out too late. Jeff, you see that she gets home at a decent hour."

"Yes, sir," Jeff sounded a little overwhelmed. Maybe it was his first date too. Sally felt sorry for him.

"We might as well run along," Jean sounded desperately calm.

The door closed behind them, and Sally went back to put on her own dress, a rose-red crepe with a sweetheart neckline and swirling skirt. She wanted to be ready the minute Al rang, so that she could rescue him from dad's corny folk music. When it had been Scotty calling for her, she had never worried about her folks.

The bell rang and Sally went down as quickly as she decently could, hoping feverishly that Rick wouldn't say anything to him about Jean, and that her father would be properly reserved. Apparently both of them had exhausted their efforts on Jeff. Dad told Al to sit down, and when Sally appeared, Rick was reading a book in the corner, occasionally looking up sidewise at the hero.

Al seemed impressed in a shy way at Sally's appearance. He rose as she came into the room and looked as if he'd be glad to get started. Even dad's glance was approving.

"Don't be too late," he reminded her, but to Al he said only, "Glad to have met you," in a man-to-man tone.

So they were finally off. Al had his father's car for the evening, and he was nervous about it. If the fender was crushed, or paint knocked off, he wouldn't get it again. He worried about getting from Juniper Lane to the high school, and fussed about parking the car until Sally was bored. She had never thought Al was scintillating, and now she was sure she was right. It was different when Scotty talked about his car!

There were mobs of people in the Social Hall, and, of course, the first person she saw in the dressing room was Louise Buck, in a tawny yellow dress that accentuated her brown hair and eyes. But tonight even Louise couldn't spoil the evening. It was funny what a comfortable secure feeling it gave Sally to be here with Al.

Louise looked her up and down with an attentive interest that Sally didn't like, and laid a friendly hand on her arm.

"Who are you with, Sally?" she asked.

Sally disengaged her arm and said coolly, "Al Carter." Not for anything would she give Louise the satisfaction of telling that she was with Scotty.

"Al Carter!" Louise squealed flatteringly. "The basketball star! Oh, isn't he simply wonderful?"

"Just simply!" Sally agreed, wondering how she could manage a dance with Scotty. Mostly you danced with the boy you came with, unless the crowd agreed among themselves to trade. And she'd rather not have the dance than let Louise know she wanted it.

"They've got programs tonight," Louise remarked, touching up her mouth.

"Oh?" Program dances were fun. Sally hoped Al had enough sense to fill hers. She could hear the orchestra playing the opening dance and her feet began to twitch. With a snap of her compact she slipped out before Louise was ready to leave.

Al was waiting, looking sheepish and uncertain, when she came back to the dance floor.

"Here's your program." He thrust it at her awkwardly, and Sally scanned it hastily. He had traded the fifth dance with Scotty; third with Jeff Sutton — that was good; seventh with Bill Nixon. A couple of other dances were circle mix-ups. This might be fun after all!

"O.K.?" he asked.

"Fine!"

It was a lucky thing they had programs, Sally discovered, within ten steps. Al was no dancer. He was stiff on his feet and uncertain about the rhythm, pushing her erratically around the floor. And he was no conversationalist. His words came out haltingly, as if his mind were all on his feet. Sally, feeling like a dud, couldn't think of a thing to say. Furiously, she found herself thinking, This is all Scotty's fault. With him she didn't have to talk, and he could dance well — and — oh, he was just more fun than this goon, even if Al could play basketball!

As the dance ended, Sally looked over Al's shoulder to face Millie and Eddie Lansing. They all stopped together.

"Sally, darling!" Millie cried vivaciously. "How perfectly wonderful to see you! I want you to know

Eddie Lansing."

Eddie was looking into Sally's eyes with a compelling admiration that left her a little dizzy. She couldn't remember when anyone had looked at her like that. Scotty never had.

She introduced the other couple to Al, and Eddie said with appropriate hopefulness, "Have you got a dance left to trade?"

Al acted confused and studied the program.

"Sixth?"

Eddie immediately wrote in his name, smiled magnetically at Sally, and said, "We'll be seeing you," as he took his partner by the arm and moved off to find their next partners. Sally watched him go. He was certainly attractive, dark and slim and very polished. The sixth dance was going to be interesting.

The next dance was a circle mix-up, and Sally drew a perfect stranger who danced even worse than Al. Oddly enough, it took the edge off her annoyance. That could have happened, even if she'd come with Scotty. Her partner seemed so much more unhappy than Sally that she was moved to make an effort at conversation, and it gave her a surprising sense of social success when he looked grateful.

When she met Al again, she determined to try to talk to him more, and salvage something out of the evening besides a dance with Scotty, if possible. He still had little to say, but he looked as if he liked her.

They met Jean and Jeff beside the drinking fountain, as prearranged. Jean was as casual as ever, but Sally could see the suppressed excitement in her eyes. She moved onto the dance floor with dreams in her eyes, and Sally hoped Al's dancing wouldn't disillusion her too much.

As the fifth dance approached, Sally found herself getting excited. That was ridiculous. Keep yourself calm, she reminded herself. It's only Scotty.

He and Louise were late. She waited with Al at the agreed spot until the orchestra had swung through the music once, before they appeared. That was most unflattering. By the time she moved onto the floor with Scotty she felt cross.

" Hi, Sally! " he said genially, his arm falling around her waist as he led her onto the floor.

" Hi," responded Sally coolly.

" How's life treating you these days? "

" Why should you care? "

" Neighborly interest, that's all."

Sally was silent. This kind of chatter wasn't leading anywhere. She was going to say something she'd be sorry for — she could feel it coming on.

" Al is awfully nice," she remarked.

" That's good. So is Louise."

" Well, if you like her type." There it was. Sally bit her lip, exasperated with herself.

" Any reason why I shouldn't? " he asked.

" Oh, no. None at all! " Sally looked over his shoulder, and Louise drifted past with Al, just then, and gave Scotty a warm smile. " Only we used to have fun together." Sally murmured.

" Yeah," he assented.

It was almost over. Sally felt a sudden desperation. She looked at him with intent, persuasive eyes. " How about bridge next Saturday with Becky and Bill? "

He shook his head. " Can't make it, Sally. Sorry."

She was seething inside as he took her back to Al. A fine waste of time that was! Thank goodness, she had the dance with Eddie Lansing to look forward to.

Eddie was a very, very good dancer, and the music was appropriately sentimental. He looked down at her and grinned as if he thought she w s cute, and that comforted her sore heart. He didn't talk much, but she got the idea that he liked her dancing and her company. And when the music ended, he said, with a confidential pressure on her hand, "You'll be seeing me again, Sally."

They rejoined Millie and Al, and for a few minutes things seemed very gay. They were all giggling when Scotty and Louise strolled by. Sally saw Scotty's eyes move from Millie to Eddie to her. But there was no expression on his face as he stepped onto the floor with Louise.

For the rest of the dance she sparkled at Al, tried to make him feel that he was the light of the evening. He knew all the proper things to do, even if he did seem a little awkward. After the dance they found Jean and Jeff, and the four of them went to the Ranch House. Sally was pleased to see Scotty and Louise in one corner, and Millie and Eddie waved from another. It was fun to be out with someone again.

And although Al left her with rather inept thanks for the evening, and no mention of another date, still the night had been successful. She had met Eddie. She was through with Scotty for good. And it was almost comforting to let him go at last.

CHAPTER
TEN

A LL of a sudden the tempo of the year seemed to
quicken. The Thanksgiving holidays were gone in a
gust of rain and sleet, December came in on a driving
snow storm, and winter was here. Sally loved the blow-
ing drama of the storm, and when it was over, the
bushes were fringed with snow and the black outlines
of the gaunt trees were streaked and softened with
white.

The music classes and the chorus at the high school
were working on their Christmas choral program. Listening to the music that filtered through the halls, Sally
was reminded vividly of other happy seasons when the
high-school singing was a festive prologue to the Christmas celebration that meant so much to the Burnabys.
Now she regretted her earlier lack of interest.

Jean was having a wonderful time. Miss Tappan had
discovered her talent for the piano, and had asked her
if she would accompany the rehearsals during the early
weeks. Jean loved playing for the chorus, and she was
finding that she knew and liked lots of people. Again
Sally felt as if she were lagging behind her sister.

After Christmas she would do something about it, she
determined, with unaccustomed decision. The annual
operetta would be coming up and probably there would

be tryouts for the chorus. For now, the best thing to do was to concentrate on Christmas at home as much as she could.

"What I want to get for mother is a waffle iron," said Jean, meditatively, sitting cross-legged on the poppy-print bedspread two weeks after Thanksgiving. "But the kind I like costs about fifteen dollars — and here I am with debts to pay and all the other presents to get —"

Sally was polishing her loafers energetically.

"I was going to look for a jersey housecoat," she said gloomily. "They all cost so much I don't see how I'll have enough even if I sit fourteen hours a day from now to New Year's. Money! It's a nuisance!"

Jean climbed off the bed to look at her calendar again.

"The chorus is taking an awful lot of time," she brooded. "They have to rehearse every afternoon and I said I'd play for them."

"We could get the waffle iron together," said Sally suddenly. "And then we could get a housecoat for her birthday, or something."

Jean drew a deep breath. "That would be fine. I could manage that without cutting out the school things. What are you getting dad?"

"Records," said Sally. "I thought of some I think he'll be crazy about. And a book about dogs for Ricky. But what about Jimmy? It's so hard to think of something for a six-year-old boy, with all of Ricky's things around!"

"More track for his train," said Jean. "He wants it to run at least twice around his room."

"I might do that too," said Sally. "We could get him yards of track, if we both got some."

"Why don't you?" suggested Jean agreeably. "What about Betsy?"

"I've got a book about acting," said Sally. "That was easy. You know she thinks she wants to be an actress."

There was a small conscientious knock at the door, and Betsy poked her head in with a self-conscious grin.

"I couldn't help hearing what you said, Sally," she explained frankly. "I didn't know you were going to be talking about my present."

Sally looked up with annoyance, and then it faded. Betsy looked so honest and so tickled to have found out a secret innocently and so thrilled with Christmas talk. Why spoil it?

"What's on your mind, Bets?"

"I just can't think what to get mother!" worried Betsy, sitting down and wrapping her pink chenille bathrobe around her knees. "I've got a dollar for her present, and she's got perfume and soap and lots of handkerchiefs —"

"Why not a plant?" suggested Sally helpfully. "She'd love an African violet."

Betsy's round face glowed with delight. "That's a wonderful idea, Sally!" She rushed off to write it down, and Sally felt a pleasant warmth around her own heart at Betsy's appreciation.

"I wish I could decide about Scotty and Millie," Sally went on with her planning.

"I thought you were going to forget about Scotty," Jean looked surprised.

"I was — I am. But he's right here in the block, and we've always exchanged something silly for Christmas, and I hate to be the one to break it off —"

"I would certainly skip Millie," said Jean scornfully. Sally resented the implication in her tone.

"I don't know." She was still prickly about Millie. Even though she didn't like her much, she had a strong sense of loyalty, and she knew Millie considered her a friend.

"Well," said Jean, "I still can't stand her. And you know mother doesn't like her."

Sally tossed her head. "I guess I'm old enough to choose my own friends," she stated positively, "and it's a good thing that mother is smart enough to know it."

Jean looked at her shrewdly.

"You can choose her if you really want her," she agreed, in an if-you-ask-me tone, "but I don't get it. She isn't your type, and when you've been with her you sound like her — if that's what you want. Sooner or later, you'll run into trouble with her. Take it from me!"

"Why should I?" Sally snapped, thoroughly incensed with unwanted advice. "Sophomores!" she muttered, with an inflection that said plainly, "Know-it-all!" The irritation on both sides was more cutting because of their recent congeniality. Jean flushed and opened her mouth, just as a knock at the door startled both girls. Mrs. Burnaby came in to distribute clean laundry.

"Some of these need mending, Sally," she remarked. "These are your socks, Jean. Holes." She laid the clothes on both beds and sat down in the red corduroy armchair for a minute.

"The Careys are going to Florida the week before Christmas," she said. "Mrs. Carey wondered if you'd be interested in taking care of their house plants while they're away. She says it's worth ten dollars to her if you'll go in twice a week and see that they are watered and sprayed."

"I should say!" Sally accepted. Her mother looked none too certain.

"I thought perhaps you had enough to do, but I hated to refuse her," she demurred.

"We can do it," said Jean positively.

"Well —" hesitated Mrs. Burnaby, "I don't want to have to do it myself!"

"Why, mother, how you talk!" Sally grinned. "Tell her Jean and I will be delighted to take the job. No trouble at all!"

Her mother nodded. "All right then. And that reminds me of something I've been intending to say." The girls looked up. "I don't want to see you getting so overwrought about earning money that you cut out more important things."

"I know, mother," began Jean, "but surely watering a few plants —"

"The Careys' plants won't be so much," her mother agreed, "but there are other things. Sometimes I think you're overdoing — your dispositions are getting edgy and it's not worth it."

Jean looked stubborn. Sally stared at the floor.

"Well, if there isn't enough money to go around," Jean pointed out, "and we can earn three or four dollars a week or so —"

"And lose sleep and temper and social life, I suppose it's an even exchange?"

"Well — no. But we haven't missed much —"

"The last few Sundays at St. Paul's, and that party at Joyce's, and a movie date for Sally," her mother pointed out. "That wouldn't amount to so much, except for all the quarreling that seems to go with it. Money isn't that important."

"O.K.," conceded Jean. "After Christmas we'll take it easy. After we pay what we owe."

"That's part of the trouble," said their mother. "It's

[107]

not healthy to owe it first and pay it afterward. Summer and holidays will be a better time to earn money than to try to crowd it into your school year with all the things there are to do."

She went out and Sally looked at Jean guiltily. They had been totaling up their finances, and it was baffling how much they had gone into debt since they had begun to earn money. Where had it all gone?

"Four dollars a week for lunches and carfare and dues," Sally repeated the figures, checking off items as she added. "I never seem to have more than small change left, with lunches costing the way they do. And ten dollars a month for clothes, except big things like coats." She frowned over her list, trying to find the discrepancy. "That used to be all right. But then I got those stadium boots, and that gold bangle bracelet to go with my red dress — but I was getting from three to five dollars a week from sitting! Oh, that sweater set in November! And the handbag! I keep forgetting. But I've got only ten dollars left altogether, and my December clothes allowance is gone — and the weekly money I'll need anyway."

"I've only got five," said Jean regretfully, "and I bought those things for the football dance. I still owe mother for the shoes — and all my Christmas shopping to do. But I just had to have that new Dickens book. And there was all that piano music!"

Sally studied her calendar. "I should make another ten dollars before the end of the year with these sitting dates," she calculated. "If we're careful, we could get by. And then the money from the Careys —"

"Maybe we could carry sandwiches for a while," suggested Jean. "We could save a couple of dollars a week that way."

"That would help," Sally agreed. "I have a feeling we won't have as much time to sit after Christmas anyway — with the operetta coming up in February and everything — "

Jean's mouth was a tight line.

"I'll work every minute I can get through vacation," she determined, "but as soon as I'm in the clear, I'm through until summer. Imagine what dad would say!"

Sally giggled. She could imagine.

"I'd like to feel as if I could turn down a sitting date when I want to," she said. "That's going to be my New Year's resolution."

The next two weeks flew past. The shops were blazoned for Christmas, and down on the Square the street lights were already framed in translucent giant bells. On one of her sitting dates on a Saturday afternoon Sally took the Clark twins down to see Santa Claus.

Kate had written that she was still planning to go to Conover and that she'd be home in another week. Now all Sally had to do was to write to the college herself. She'd do that the minute school was out.

She had found a handkerchief with a Black-eyed Susan embroidered in petit point in the corner and "Kate" written in large letters across the stems. It looked just like Kate, and Sally knew she'd love it.

She and Jean spent most of one Saturday morning at King's, choosing the waffle iron for mother and the records for father. In the record department they ran into Rick, who looked at them as if he didn't recognize his sisters. When they spoke to him, he was embarrassed.

"Christmas shopping?" Sally teased.

"Yeah!" The clerk had returned to give him his change and a large paper bag, which he clutched as if he wanted to conceal it. Without another word, he backed away and ducked out.

"Secrets!" giggled Sally, amused at how hard it was for Burnabys to organize their Christmas without finding out each other's plans.

She and Jean were sobered to find that they had only five dollars apiece left, after the morning's shopping. With care they could get through the year, perhaps. They were diligently making sandwiches every night, wrapping them in waxed paper to carry the next morning. That helped a lot. But there were so many extras! A dollar to the school Christmas fund for charity. Christmas seals. Christmas basket fund at St. Paul's.

Thank goodness they could collect the ten dollars from the Careys sometime after the holidays.

Al called for a Saturday night movie, but Sally had to sit. She hadn't dared to refuse the job, when she needed the money so badly. But she was genuinely regretful. Only two more weeks, and she'd be through with this grind.

Then school was over and Christmas was less than a week away. The Careys left on Friday night, after a conversation with Sally and Jean about the house plants.

Mrs. Carey was a rather regal-looking lady, with snow-white hair and a mouth which she herself considered firm. Mother claimed that Mrs. Carey was very goodhearted, and would do anything for a neighbor. But Sally was none too sure.

"These are the plants, girls," said Mrs. Carey, without a trace of a smile. There was an enormous basket of ivy in the sunroom that stood thirty inches high. Dozens of ivy strands cascaded to the floor. A philodendron at the opposite end of the room had grown until it was twined around the windows like drapery.

"The philodendron should be watered twice a week," said their employer. "The ivy must be sprayed twice a week, on both sides of the leaves. The container will take two quarts of water."

Then there were two variegated ivies on the mantel, an African violet on the desk, begonias in the kitchen window, plants in every beautifully decorated room upstairs.

"Do you still think you can do it?" demanded Mrs. Carey, the ghost of a smile on her firm mouth. Sally looked at Jean and nodded. This was big business. "Just so we don't do it wrong," she said dubiously. "Those big things in the sunroom — it must take a lifetime to grow them like that."

"Pretty nearly," said Mrs. Carey dryly, without elaboration. Sally wondered fleetingly what she meant. "There isn't much chance of going wrong," she added, "if you just water them twice a week, as much as the containers will hold without dripping."

The girls were thoughtful as they went home. This was more of a responsibility than they had realized.

"I'll take it Tuesdays and you take it Fridays," Jean suggested. "But let's remind each other."

"I'll put it on my calendar," said Sally, making notes for two weeks ahead.

Sally spent Saturday morning making two batches of fudge, finding suitable boxes for them, and wrapping the packages. If Scotty came around to say Merry Christmas, she'd have something for him. If not, she'd eat it herself.

Kate got in on Saturday afternoon. When Sally talked to her on the phone, it seemed as if she'd never left — she was still Kate, gay and fun to talk to, anxious to have Sally come over, full of questions about what was happening at school.

Lounging on Kate's green-and-blue plaid gingham bed, Sally tried to figure out just what it was that made Kate such a grand person. It wasn't her looks, which were average: she was medium tall, with a nice figure, brown hair that swept smoothly back from a center part into a roll around her head, blue eyes, and a wide expressive mouth. It must be something deeper than looks.

Kate turned to her just then. "I've been hearing all sorts of things about the crowd, since I went away," she said in the confidential way that Sally always enjoyed. "Marian wrote me about Louise. She said she didn't like her much. But that was all she said. What's wrong with Scotty?"

For the first time since Kate had gone away, Sally felt as if she could talk out the problem with someone. As she spoke, thoughts ran through Sally's mind, supplementing the story itself. It was lucky so many weeks had passed since that unhappy party at Scotty's house. Now she could tell the whole tale without a quiver. Last October she would have cried on Kate's shoulder.

"Well," remarked Kate at the end, "you know what I think? I think he's getting restless. He's felt kind of tied to his mother's apron strings, and now is the time he wants to break away. You'd never know he felt that way — he was always so casual and easygoing — but I had that feeling last summer. Mrs. Scott was always making him go to a family party when the gang wanted to have a picnic or something. Ted mentioned it once."

"He can break away all he wants to," said Sally bitterly. "I'm through."

Kate nodded. "I think you're wise to forget him,

Sally. No one can hold a boy when he feels that way. He's nice, of course. But nobody's that nice. The smartest thing you ever did was to go to that football dance with Al Carter. And who knows — if Scotty thought he was losing you, instead of getting away from you — it might give him a new idea!"

By the time Sally went home she was contented with her life. Now how could Kate always make her feel that way? She tried again to analyze the subtle charm of personality. No matter what you told her, Kate was never shocked or disapproving. She just seemed to understand how you felt. She was amused when you were, sympathetic when you were hurt, delighted with good news.

Perhaps mother had been right when she said it might be good for Sally to get along without Kate for a while. She had never been so much aware of Kate's finer qualities. How did you develop a personality like that? Just as she was falling asleep the answer came to her: Concentrate, always, on the other person and his feelings, instead of on yourself.

If she had done that with Jean she would have got along with her much earlier than she did. And even when she concentrated on Scotty, it was her own feelings that she put first, trying always to make him feel the way she did, instead of letting him go his own way. Perhaps she could still do something about it.

Kate organized a sleigh ride the first thing, for Tuesday night. The whole crowd was there — the old crowd that Sally had always enjoyed. Sally felt like herself again with them. Scotty was more like his old self too, bantering and cheerful. And this time she could laugh at his jokes and turn to Glen as if Scotty were someone she hardly knew. When the ride was over, she busied herself in Kate's kitchen, passing out food and cocoa. When she sat down with her own plate, it was with Glen and Marian that she talked and laughed.

By the end of the evening she had a feeling that Scotty was a little puzzled. But she couldn't be sure.

W ITH all the flurry of preparations, Sally had almost forgotten what a magical time Christmas was. But the day after Kate's sleigh ride she woke up full of ideas for decorating the house. And, as the wreaths went up in the windows and the greens outlined the doorways, as Jimmy and Betsy lovingly set out the crèche and Ricky built the fire, decorated with pine branches and cones, to be lighted on Christmas Eve, she remembered, as she did every year, that no other occasion all year through was quite as important as their family Christmas.

The holiday belonged to the Burnaby children, and they relished every moment of preparation. Now that Sally could drive, she took all of them out to find the tree, visiting half a dozen lots and examining dozens of trees critically before making their choice. When they returned, exulting, for lunch, they brought the very best tree in the whole town, according to Jimmy and Rick. The girls felt the same way.

The day before Christmas was reserved for decorating the tree. The girls spent the morning putting the last touches on the house: every bedroom had a bit of Christmas in it. Christmas cards stood along the sunroom window sills, and Jimmy walked around and around the room, relishing each card as if it had come to him.

Mother made doughnuts for lunch that day, a very special treat that marked important events.

"Oh, boy," sighed Betsy, reaching for her third. "Don't we have the most wonderful food?"

After lunch Ricky fitted the tree into the standard, and the girls got out the ornaments and lights. Every ornament had a special meaning. Mother used to remark wistfully that it would be nice to have a blue and silver Christmas, or to do the tree all in green and gold, but every time she tried a special scheme, either one of the younger children would be heartbroken at the absence of a favorite Santa Claus or Sally couldn't bear to omit any of the ornaments Scotty had given her. Ever since kindergarten, when he had proudly brought over a tiny yarn Santa for Sally's tree, he had given her a new ornament at Christmas time. Once it was half a dozen snowballs. In junior high school, he had painstakingly cut out wooden gingerbread men and rocking horses and stars, and painted them himself.

The tree was lighted, the candelabra gleamed on the mantelpiece, the Christmas music was arranged on the piano. Ricky lighted the fire and the five Burnabys sat down to drink milk and eat the first pieces of Christmas fruitcake. Mother joined them, and father came in five minutes later. Jean drank the last swallow of milk in her glass, and went to the piano.

"Play 'The Friendly Beasts,'" said Betsy. This had been her favorite carol since she was three years old. As Jean played the ancient melody, they all began to sing, and one by one they gathered about the piano, as she went on with "The Holly and the Ivy." Sally carried the descant, and mother sang the contralto part, while the others sang the old English melody. Mother leaned forward to turn the pages over Jean's shoulder.

"How about 'Bring the torch, Jeannette, Isabella'?"

After that they sang "Dame, Get Up and Bake Your Pies," and mother looked at the clock.

"Very appropriate," she said. "This dame had better get up and bake some pies if we want dinner in an hour."

"My goodness, I've still got presents to wrap!" exclaimed Sally. With instructions to Jimmy and Betsy to stay away, she flew upstairs while Jean went out to set the table.

They always had turkey on Christmas Eve, so that Christmas Day would be free for relaxation and friends. A Burnaby special plum pudding, which never failed to blaze handsomely when it was lighted, was ready on the sideboard, a sprig of holly stuck into its crest.

Sally had never felt so united with her family as she glanced around the circle of faces at the table. What did it matter if Kate and Scotty came or went? She had her family. She glanced toward the tree in the window and the piles of Christmas presents, and thought she really must be growing up: she was much more excited to see how the others would like her presents than about the ones she was going to get.

After the dinner dishes were done, there was another round of carols, and then Betsy and Jimmy went off to bed, the starry promise of Christmas Day surrounding them like a halo. Ricky was going caroling with a group of boys in the neighborhood, and Sally and Jean planned to attend Midnight Mass at St. Paul's. Mother and dad couldn't go because of the younger children. But Sally loved it.

Sitting in the little church banked with greens and lighted with dozens of candles, Sally felt almost entirely at peace with herself. The magic hour of midnight on Christmas Eve always had seemed to bring her understanding of the past year's mistakes and strength for the year to come, but never as clearly as this time.

To the stirring rhythm of "Adeste Fideles," the choir swung down the aisle behind the triumphant cross. The priest at the altar, in richly embroidered robes of white, read the beautiful words of the service in a voice as musical as an organ. And everyone in the church moved forward to the Communion rail while the choir sang old French and Bohemian and English carols.

Sally felt entirely happy as she returned to her place. "Thank you, God, for Christmas," she murmured on her knees. When they came out of the church at one thirty, snow was falling — a soft, quiet fall that made a picture of the night. Christmas was here again.

The family was up early the next morning. Sally heard Jimmy clatter up and down stairs at some unspeakable hour. She opened a drowsy eye — seven o'clock! What made children so vigorous? She went back to sleep.

At ten she woke again, suddenly excited about the day.

"Merry Christmas, Jean!" She shook her sister and went to wash her face and brush her teeth. Then she slipped into her quilted housecoat and warm slippers, brushed her hair hastily, and ran down the stairs. Ricky was ahead of her, of course. Betsy had been up as long as Jimmy. The living room was already littered with bright wrapping paper and glittering strings and ribbons. Dad was beginning to pick them up and stuff them into the crackling fire.

"Merry Christmas!" cried mother.

"You should *see* what we got!" screamed Betsy and Jimmy. Ricky was too absorbed in his ice skates and knife, books and basketball, to notice his older sisters.

Sally had thought she was past the childish excitement of Christmas packages. But when she saw the unopened presents still under the tree she felt a familiar tingle of anticipation.

"Let's open the things before we eat!" she cried, finding her pile. Mother was just unwrapping the waffle iron.

"Wonderful!" she cried. "Waffles for supper tonight!" She hugged the girls enthusiastically. Dad was putting his new records on the machine: fifteenth-century English carols, sung with a descant. "I've been looking for this album for years," he said, pleased.

"It just came back into print for this season," Sally told him. Really, it was such fun to buy presents for her family. They always *liked* them so much!

She finally got her own opened: an evening bag from mother, a spring housecoat, new compact, perfume from Jean, candy from Rick, nylons. "This is a wonderful Christmas!" Sally cried, looking from one to another of her family. "Betsy, you cute thing! How did you know I love handkerchiefs?"

"I thought maybe you needed one," said Betsy, terribly pleased.

Jean's gifts were just what she wanted too: a frilly slip, a housecoat, books, a fountain pen, a piano record from Rick.

And then it was time for dinner.

When dinner was over, Sally and Jean went upstairs to dress. Every year some of the neighbors dropped in on Christmas afternoon. Sally hoped this year would be no different, as she chose her favorite date dress of soft green wool with a double row of silver buttons.

"Merry Christmas!" she heard Kate's voice downstairs. Then the bell rang again. It was Scotty. Sally's hands were cold and a little shaky.

She could hear Jimmy loudly demonstrating to Scotty the parts he had got for his electric train and Betsy excitedly telling Kate about her new books. Sally took a last look in the mirror and made ready to join them. Then she paused.

Sitting down at her dressing table again, she leaned her face in her hands. "Let me do this right," she begged herself. "Let me take it easy with Scotty. Let me act the way I should — not trying to make him like me or anything."

Her cheeks were flushed as she went down the stairs, but she felt as if she knew how she wanted to act. Scotty was on the floor, working with Jimmy's train. Kate and Betsy were chatting on the couch.

"Merry Christmas, Kate!" Sally cried. "Merry Christmas, Scotty! Isn't this a wonderful day?" They both returned her greeting and Kate picked up a small package she had laid on the desk.

"Yours is under the tree," said Sally, burrowing among the still unopened gifts. She pulled out Scotty's present and handed it to him.

"Sally, what a love of a handkerchief!" exclaimed Kate. Sally was examining Kate's present with delight: a tiny dial telephone for her charm bracelet.

"This is precious," she said, holding it in the palm of her hand. "I've never seen one before. Where on earth did you find it?"

"Up at school," said Kate.

Scotty dropped a package in her lap with elaborate unconcern. "Just a little thing I hemstitched in my spare time," he said.

"If I can't use it, I'll save it for the rummage sale," Sally promised, opening it with fingers that fumbled. Scotty was already sampling his present.

"The best fudge you ever made," he said, putting two pieces in his mouth. Jimmy reached for some, and Sally said with a grin: "You don't have to give it all to the Burnabys either. There's some for them in the candy dish."

She looked at the box in her lap and stifled a gasp. It was a little silver bell for the Christmas tree, with a holly wreath engraved around the edge — the prettiest thing he had given her! With a tingle of elation, she hung it high on the tree. As she turned to say something

[121]

appreciative, a faint wariness on his face made her hesitate. She turned back to the tree, fixing the tiny bell in place. Careful now, she warned herself, or this will be the last ornament you'll ever get from him!

"Pretty nice, Mr. Scott," she remarked, as she came back from the tree. "Right in the old tradition, and welcome. Don't make yourself sick on that fudge. How about some fruitcake to go with it, and a couple of dozen cookies?"

"O.K.," said Scotty, as indifferently as ever. "How about it?"

"You might find something in the dining room," Sally told him, sitting down by Kate. "You've got feet, haven't you?"

Scotty grinned as if he felt at home again and disappeared toward the dining room.

The bell rang again and Millie appeared, her hands full of packages. The fresh-fallen snow on her hair and veil accented her lovely coloring.

"Merry Christmas, folks!" she said, a little shyly. Sally took her wraps and led her toward the circle around the fire.

Millie had a present for each of the Burnabys, and Sally felt slightly embarrassed at the modest box of fudge she was giving Millie in return.

"This is the loveliest family," she sighed, sitting back and watching them. Sally was puzzled. After all, Millie had two brothers herself.

"Christmas just isn't like this at our house," the girl said with a bitter edge to her words. "It seems like a time for families —"

She broke off and stared into the fire, until Sally laid her own present in her lap.

"Why, Sally, how nice!" Millie exclaimed. She didn't

eat any candy, though, and Sally wondered if she'd made a mistake. Why hadn't she got her something like a handkerchief? Dad was putting on his records again, and Sally was pleased to see their guests listening with quiet interest.

"We always play records on Christmas afternoon," she explained.

"I wish we did," said Millie, a little ruefully. "My folks went to a party on the other side of town. But I said I was going to come over here, and I'm glad I did."

Sally caught her mother's eye. Mother looked unexpectedly sympathetic. Maybe now she'd know what Sally meant when she said Millie needed her.

Twilight had already settled outside, and dad lighted candles on the mantel and passed mulled cider and cake. And then it was time to go. Kate and Scotty made the first move, and Millie joined them as if she hated to leave. Sally wondered, as she closed the door behind them, if Scotty would be seeing Louise today. But it didn't matter now. He had come to their house — and he had given her a Christmas bell.

"I'm awfully tired," said Betsy unexpectedly, flopping back on the couch. "I think I'll go to bed." Her cheeks were flushed and her eyes looked a little glazed. Sally looked at her in concern. Betsy was so untiringly active! Mother seemed concerned too, as she placed an expert hand on Betsy's forehead.

"Too much Christmas," she said, as she led her away and helped her up the stairs. But her face was more serious than her words. Sally watched them go and then stared into the fire, not thinking of much except the happiness of the day.

Mother came down again, wearing a worried frown.

"It's probably only excitement and fatigue," she

said, as if she didn't believe it herself, " but I think I'll talk to Dr. Neal anyhow."

"You don't really think it's anything serious? " asked Sally, looking up quickly.

"You never know about these things," said her mother, with uncharacteristic pessimism.

≫≫≫≫≫≫≫≫≫≫≫≫≫≫≫≫≫≫≫≫≫≫≫≫≫≫≫≫≫≫≫≫≫

CHAPTER TWELVE

TOO much Christmas was what the doctor thought too, the next day. Betsy was to stay in bed and keep warm and quiet — a touch of flu. " But you never can tell what flu can develop into," he said amiably. " Don't take any chances."

So Sally stopped worrying. Anyone could get flu — and Betsy was so strong and healthy, she'd be over it in no time at all. Sally had other things on her mind the last week of vacation. She took care of the house plants on Friday, and was agreeably surprised to find that the job took less than an hour.

Kate wanted her to have lunch downtown and go to a movie on Tuesday. But Sally had already promised the day to Mrs. Dale, at the other end of the block. A month ago she would have felt bitterly cheated to miss the day with Kate. Now she could tell her cheerfully about the sitting date, and, more important, she didn't mind keeping it.

She was divided between pleasure at earning three dollars and apprehension over how the children would behave. Lately, though, she had been developing a good technique of persuasion and distraction, and taking care of them had been more fun than trouble.

Promptly at ten she rang the Dales' doorbell, wincing as she heard the screams inside. Mrs. Dale looked harried when she opened the door, her hat already on, a few wisps of hair straggling out at the edges.

"I'm leaving right now," she said, almost in a whisper. "I hate to tell you, Sally, but they're not very coöperative today. Sometimes I think there must be some mistake in the book I've been using: the children just don't respond the way it says they will. I'll be back at five and the lunch is written out on the pad in the kitchen, and the things are all in the icebox."

Sally found the children with little difficulty. They were quarreling noisily in the playroom on the second floor. Benjy had Susan's Christmas doll at arm's length over his head and she was making ready to hit him with one of Timmy's heavy blocks, which he threatened to parry with the doll. When Susan, who was four, saw Sally, she stopped the attack and began to cry.

"Where's my mother?" she sobbed. "Go away. I don't want you. I want my mother."

Sally rescued the doll and gave it to her. She sent the two boys into another room alone, and closed Susan's door until the screams stopped. Benjy and Timmy were willing to play with some new blocks and Lincoln logs, and she left them constructing a fort quite happily. Then she went back to Susan.

The little girl was looking forlornly out of the window, sobbing quietly. When Sally put an arm around her, she was violently repulsed.

"How would you like to hear the story about Little Red Riding Hood?" she asked. Susan eyed her suspiciously, then surrendered. They sat on one of the beds, and Sally began the story. Halfway through, Susan was snuggling up as she listened, the sobs entirely forgotten.

"Read another," she demanded, when Sally finished.

[126]

Sally read about the three bears and the gingerbread man and Chicken Little. After a while, the boys crept in and listened too. By lunch time they were easily persuaded to put the toys away and wash their hands.

Susan balked at the menu, but Sally kept control of the situation. "There isn't anything else to eat," she said firmly, serving the boys who were too hungry to argue. Susan pouted and sulked and tipped over her milk. In the end she admitted she was hungry and ate all her lunch after the boys had gone up to take their naps.

"Now read some more!" she demanded expectantly. Sally shook her head. "After your nap," she said. An inspiration struck her. "Look!" she picked up the alarm clock in the kitchen. "When it's time to get up the bell will ring. You listen for it. All by itself, out of this clock, the bell will ring. Then you can get up and I'll take you all for a ride on your sled."

Susan looked suspicious, then credulous. A self-ringing bell was even more of a novelty than a story. And a ride with a sled in the snow — she gave up and went off for her nap.

Sally sat down for a bite to eat, thinking about the children. She almost never had any trouble with them now, no matter how unpromising the beginning of the day might be. Learning how to manage them was the first achievement she could remember that was due entirely to her own initiative and ingenuity.

Take Susan, for instance. Earlier in the year Sally had thought her homely and unattractive, but when she was telling her stories, or helping her with her meals, or listening to her chatter, Sally found herself growing fond of the little girl.

"It's a funny thing," Sally said to herself, munching

her peanut-butter sandwich and drinking a second glass of milk; "Timmy is adorable, actually — but I like Susan just as well — "

It *was* funny. Few of the children she had taken care of had looked very appealing when she first met them, yet they had soon developed special individualities. She had never thought she cared for children much, before she had started this sitting program. But one of the high lights of the year was the day she had taught Susan how to button her own coat. She could still remember her excitement as she watched the little fingers struggling with the buttonholes, trying over and over, until they mastered the intricacies of slipping a button in and out instead of tearing it off.

It would be kind of fun to teach kids, Sally thought. And she jumped with the explosiveness of the idea. It was the answer she had been groping for all year — the answer to the high-school senior's biggest question: What do I want to do with my life?

Sally took especial pains with the children when they wakened, helping them with their clothes, showing them how to do things themselves. Even two-year-old Timmy found his own shoes and put them on himself. Sally could hardly wait for Mrs. Dale's astonished applause. The big moment of the day came when Susan learned to tie her own shoes. Sally showed her how to do it, and Susan watched attentively.

"Now let me do it!" she demanded. And while Sally watched in breathless suspense, the clumsy little fingers slowly pushed and pulled the stringy laces into an awkward bowknot.

"Wonderful, Susan!" cried Sally with a hug. Susan's homely little face was quite transformed at the praise.

The rest of the afternoon flew past almost unnoticed.

It took half an hour to get the three children dressed for the outdoors. By four fifteen they were ready to go out with the sled. And by four forty-five it was time to come in again and go through the whole process in reverse, knocking snow off feet, shaking and brushing it off snow suits, hanging wet things to dry. Sally felt a glow of pride in all the things she had remembered, and a small subconscious sympathy for Mrs. Dale. She was beginning to understand why Mrs. Dale had had little time to spend on her hair before she went out.

When Mrs. Dale came home, the three flung themselves, screaming and chattering, upon her. "Sally read us stories." "And Susan ate all her lunch." "And Timmy's mitten was lost, and Benjy found it." Sally waited for someone to tell how much they had learned about dressing, but no one mentioned it. Finally she said casually, "And Susan tied her own shoes, Mrs. Dale!"

"Did she?" The fond mother beamed on Susan proudly. "Isn't that fine? She's been doing that for the past week, Sally, and we think it's pretty smart."

Sally was deflated. What was the point in teaching if they knew all the answers beforehand? But some of her first exhilaration clung, and as she walked home she thought of Susan with interest and a little fondness, even if the child had fooled her by knowing all the time how to tie her own shoes.

When she got home, she found Betsy standing before her mirror, pinning her braids around her head.

"Aren't you supposed to be in bed?" she asked.

"I'm perfectly well," Betsy snapped. "Just a little tired, that's all, and I get more tired of staying in bed. I just hafta get up and move around *once* in a while!"

She couldn't be too sick, feeling like that, Sally thought. Tonight she must talk over this business of college with Kate. Now that she had thought of teaching, there would be new angles to consider.

She tried it out on her family at dinner.

"What do you think I ought to do after college, dad?" she asked, as he was dishing out the spaghetti and meat balls.

"How should I know?" he asked. That was his stock reply to questions beginning, "What do you think I should do?" and Sally found it irritating. What were parents for, anyway, if they couldn't tell you things you wanted to know? She refused to say any more. As the big wooden bowl of salad was being passed, dad took up the unanswered question again.

"After fifteen years of patiently trying to make you children *think* a little, my oldest child still wants to know what *I* think. The question is, what do *you* think, Sally?"

"Well," she was still a little irritated by the opening of the discussion, "it's kind of hard to know about your lifework without giving different things a try. But I *think* I'd like to teach — maybe."

Mother looked up eagerly. "Why, I think that would be a wonderful choice, Sally! I used to teach, and I always liked it."

"I still like it," said dad, looking pleased at his daughter's choice. "You'll never make a million dollars, but most people never make a million anyway — and it has other rewards."

Sally was satisfied. Let's not talk about it any more, she thought. That's all I wanted to know.

"I can't *imagine* being a teacher!" declared Jean, with a grimace.

"I still remember that first class I had," mother was reminiscing, and she went on with a long story about how she was afraid the boys would throw spitballs at her and how one of the girls talked back the first week and she didn't know what to do. Sally began to fret inside. That's how it was: Tell your parents one little thing and they never know when to let it alone.

"How's Betsy getting along?" asked dad.

Mother sighed. "It's almost impossible to keep her in bed, and that fever just hangs on. I don't like it."

"I'll talk to her," promised dad. "She'll have to stay put if she wants to get back to school on time." He ran a hand over his smooth sandy hair and rubbed the back of his neck, as if he was tired. Then he grinned at mother, one of those private interchanges of sympathy that Sally rarely noticed. "Quite a family!" His eyes followed Ricky, as his son excused himself and sagged down, one leg over the arm of an easy chair, with the evening funnies.

The question of teaching was forgotten, and as far as Sally was concerned, she was just as glad. She wanted to save further discussion for Kate.

"You know what!" said Sally dramatically, sitting on Kate's bed that evening. "I've finally decided what I'm going to do after college."

"What?" demanded Kate. "I'm going into journalism; I've made up my mind."

"I'm going to be a teacher!" Sally felt more elated every time she made the declaration.

"No!" Kate was astonished. "When did you think of that?"

"Just this afternoon, taking care of the Dales. I was teaching them how to put on their clothes, and Susan tied her own shoes — and it was kind of fun, watching them learn, and suddenly I knew. This was IT! I think teaching would be fun."

Kate looked thoughtful.

"You used to talk about advertising or journalism, along with me," she said.

"Well, I was thinking about it," said Sally, honestly, "mostly because you were going to do that, I guess. And it sounded kind of glamorous — the things you hear about writers and advertising men. But I never really felt as if I could do it. I just couldn't imagine myself sitting at a typewriter and writing stuff all day long. I can't even write letters — you know that!"

Kate grinned. "That I know! Well — I think you'd be a good teacher, Sally. It's not for me — but if you liked it, it could be fun. We can still go to the same school — you can take education at any of them."

"I'll get at it this week," Sally promised. "Where have you decided?"

"I still want to go to Conover, right here in the Middle West," said Kate. "I want a small school."

"I'd thought of Conover," said Sally, "ever since you first mentioned it. And dad thinks it's a good school. I'll write up there right away."

"It's pretty late," said Kate, worriedly. "I thought you were going to write before this."

"I should have," said Sally, without any particular concern, "but I kept forgetting — so many things kept coming up. But it'll be all right. Millie thinks she's going to Western State."

"I didn't think she could get in anywhere," said Kate frankly. "Your grades have to be awfully high these days."

"What Millie really wants is to get married," said Sally, with a smile. Kate looked startled. "At this age? Is she crazy?"

"Kind of," Sally agreed. "She keeps talking about

being eighteen — she's a year older than we are, you know — and what's the use of studying, just to keep house, and she isn't going to get left, the way career girls might, and stuff like that. And she isn't very happy at home."

"Well —" Kate was reflective. "It'll be fun to keep house and raise a family, naturally. But not for a couple of years yet, for heaven's sake! I wouldn't want to miss college."

"That's what I keep telling her," said Sally. "Only she doesn't want to study, and she says that would take all the fun out of college for her."

"Where is Scotty going?" Kate dropped the question of Millie. She never seemed to want to discuss the girl.

"Last fall he was going to State University," said Sally. "Of course, I haven't had much chance to talk to him since then —"

"Ted thinks he's going to State too," said Kate. "Law."

"Life is so complicated," said Sally, musingly. "I thought senior year was going to be the most fun of all — and then you leave, and Scotty falls apart, and people keep poking at me about my career and college — and grades get more and more important. Is this what it's going to be like, being grown up? I'm not so struck with the idea."

"It's just facing all the changes at once," said Kate, as if she knew exactly what Sally meant. "I felt the same way last summer, when I found out about Harper, and Aunt Wilma died, and everything. I thought of all times to go away to school, it had to be senior year! But it's not so bad, after all. Things happen that way, I've found. Shake them up and let them settle."

"And if it isn't anything else," Sally remembered

suddenly, "someone gets sick. I guess I'd better go home. I promised I'd stay in tomorrow and play with Betsy. She won't stay in bed by herself."

She walked the short distance in the snow, feeling good in spite of herself. Now if Betsy would just get over this flu, everything would be all right. Sally smiled as she thought of her little sister. Watching Betsy grow up was like knowing her own childhood all over again. She had worn braids then; she had fussed about the braces; she had been mad about radio serials. It was silly to worry over a mild touch of flu, she kept telling herself. But just the same, she couldn't help it.

CHAPTER
THIRTEEN

>>>

THE old crowd were together again at Kate's New
Year's Eve party and Sally had more fun than at
any time since last year. Kate knew how to plan a party:
she had games, and there were horns and whistles and
noisemakers and new records and practical jokes —
everything.

Now that she could take Scotty or leave him, Sally had
fun with everyone. Once, she was pleased to notice,
Scotty even looked at her, when he thought she was
turned the other way, with a sort of surprise, as if she
were someone new.

It was a perfect ending for an imperfect year. As
they shouted and sang the new year in, Sally could look
ahead with confidence, and even excitement, to what
this year would bring.

Then the holidays were over. Kate went back to
school. Jean could hardly wait until basketball games began again. The very last night of vacation, Sally spent
the evening composing a letter to Conover College and
sent it off, feeling very virtuous. One by one the problems of her senior year were being solved.

Betsy, to everyone's concern, was not much interested
in going back to school. Although she was up and
around again, she complained that her knees hurt when
she went upstairs, and then her elbows ached, and then

her feet were tired. At first it was mildly funny, but after three days of complaints mother was worried.

"I think I'll have to have Dr. Neal come in again," she declared at breakfast one morning. "It isn't like Betsy to have these miseries all the time."

"Growing pains," said dad, trying to cool his coffee so that he could drink it fast. "She'll get over it."

But mother looked thoughtful. "I'll see," she said noncommittally.

Betsy was dawdling over her breakfast. "Do I have to go to school today?" she asked. "I don't feel much like it."

Sally felt alarmed about her younger sister. "You always used to like school," she remarked. "What's wrong, Toots?"

"I just feel tired all the time."

Mother rose decisively at that point and went to the telephone. Dad grabbed his brief case and hurried off to catch a bus for an eight o'clock class. "Let me know if anything's wrong," he called as he left.

Sally lingered over her wraps, waiting to hear what her mother would report.

"Dr. Neal will be in this morning," said mother, looking more concerned than ever. "Betsy, if you're tired, go back to bed and rest."

Getting back into the routine of classes wasn't too bad that first day after the Christmas holidays. Sally decided that she would try to get into the spring operetta work, already being discussed by the whole school. Perhaps she could join the chorus or work on one of the committees. It would keep her afternoons busy.

"Have you decided about college next year?" Sally

asked Millie when they met on the bus going home. The subject was on her mind oftener since she had mailed the letter to Conover.

Millie looked sulky, as she did whenever college was mentioned.

"Mother wrote to Western State," she said, with a toss of her head that disowned the whole transaction, "but I loathe the idea, simply loathe it! Why should *I* go to college?"

"Well — it seems kind of soon to — well, I mean, get married!" said Sally, with the incredulity that she felt whenever they discussed Millie's plans. "And anyway, the boys can't — they don't want to start working so soon. How could Rod earn enough?"

"Who said anything about Rod?" Millie sniffed. "He's just a kid. But you know that man I told you about last Thanksgiving? He was in the Army and everything, and now he's got a good job in the credit department of King's. I've been seeing him pretty often. He says no more school for him. All he wants is to settle down." She looked radiant again.

The whole idea fascinated Sally, and she thought about it as they got off the bus and strolled along Juniper Lane. There was a sense of past and present, faraway and here-at-home memories, all wrapped in the fall of snow that covered the trees and houses. She loved Juniper Lane, Sally thought passionately. She loved her home and family. She didn't want to leave for years and years. Except, of course, to go to college, and then she'd always be coming back.

Millie stopped with her a minute and looked through the lighted windows, at the cozy scene of books and chairs and presence of people.

"Your home is nice," she said enviously. "All lighted

[137]

up and your family are there — at least some of them. Nobody is ever at my house when I go home except the housekeeper, and she's an old hatchet face. I think our house is a terrible place! "

She strode away pessimistically, plowing up the soft snow with her stadium boots, and Sally went in, feeling sorry for Millie, as she did so often these days, yet unqualified to help her. The knowledge that Millie relied on her was flattering, but disturbing.

"Sally?" her mother called from upstairs. "Will you start supper? I'll be down in a minute."

"How's Betsy?" Sally shouted up.

"Sick in bed. I'll be down in a minute. Put some water on to boil, please." She sounded agitated.

Sally hung up her coat, smoothed her hair, washed her hands, and set about the kitchen business. Betsy sick again? A little chill of fear crept over her. A minute later her mother joined her, bustling as if there were too many things to do.

"Dr. Neal says it's rheumatic fever," said her mother, looking drawn. Sally dropped her knife.

"Rheumatic fever!" she said. "What does that mean?"

"It means she has to stay in bed three or four months, and she *may* escape heart damage." Her mother was vigorously slicing green beans. She seemed relieved to have someone to talk it over with.

"I talked to dad when he was here at noon. But if there's one thing I've always been afraid of, it's rheumatic fever — more than polio, even. And now we've got it." She tightened her lips, as if a sharp pain passed through her.

"Four months in bed!" breathed Sally. "The poor little kid!"

As soon as the beans were finished, she went up to see Betsy.

"Hi, Bets!" she said, surprised to find her little sister looking exactly as she had looked in the morning. "It's too bad, honey, but everybody will come in to see you. We'll keep you so busy you won't even notice the time!"

Betsy was already feeling sorry for herself, and Sally's sympathy brought slow tears to her eyes.

"My Brownie troop will get way ahead of me," she wept, "and I won't pass fourth grade."

Jean came up with her condolences. "Sure you will, sugar," she patted the little girl fondly. "We'll all read to you and help you with your lessons. Why, you'll probably not want to get up, you'll get so much service, with all this family!"

Betsy's eyes began to brighten. "Can I wear your watch, Jean?" she begged.

"Sure enough," said Jean. "You can have anything you want when you're sick."

By suppertime the whole family had heard the news, and the reaction was unanimous. Betsy had been such a busy and self-reliant little girl — what on earth would she do for four months?

After supper everyone gathered in her room. Dad read her the funnies in the paper, and Ricky slipped out to the drugstore for a new comic book and a lollipop which lasted all evening. Betsy looked almost happy when, at eight thirty, she fell asleep with the radio still running.

The next day mother told the girls that she was giving up her outside activities in order to spend all her time with Betsy. "Either that or a trained nurse," she said quietly. It gave Sally a turn. Even thinking of a

[139]

nurse made Betsy's illness seem much more serious than she had supposed.

"Of course, I'll let the University Circle go, and the Garden Club," mother went on, matter-of-factly. "I don't mind at all — "

Sally knew how much her mother enjoyed friends in those clubs — and the active season for the Garden Club was just beginning. But there wasn't much Sally could do. She couldn't stay out of school long enough to take full care of the invalid. Yet she had a sobering idea of the complications the family would face this spring.

The next week was hectic. Sally and Jean hurried home every night to dance attendance on Betsy. Ricky gave up his beloved Y for a week, where he had been allowed to swim every other night after supper. Betsy had a field day.

She tinkled her little bell every thirty minutes or oftener. She was thirsty. Then she was hungry. Could she have a coke? How about a cookie? She clung to Jean's watch with tears. After all, she was sick, wasn't she? She wanted more comic books, and Ricky made countless trips to the drugstore for them.

She got bored easily and wanted someone in her room all the time. She demanded to hear the radio mystery programs that were normally forbidden. She wanted daddy to read to her for hours on end because she couldn't go to sleep. The healthy Burnabys became so worn out satisfying her whims that they grew ill-tempered with each other. By the end of the week Sally's patience began to wear thin.

"Listen," she said to Jean, behind their closed door, "we can't go on like this! We've all had enough. And mother says four months!"

"I want my watch," grumbled Jean. "I need it. Bets

could have an alarm clock."

"I feel bad about her being sick," said Sally, "but she's acting like a brat. No one is sick enough for that. I'm going to speak to mother about it."

Together they went purposefully downstairs, where mother was trying to sort laundry, losing the count again and again.

"Mother, does Betsy have to be like this?" demanded Sally, sitting on the corner of the table, one saddle shoe swinging. "Because we think she's acting terrible. I mean, keeping everyone jumping all the time."

Mother gave up the counting wearily.

"I know. It's pretty bad. She's not quite that way during the day. But when you girls get home, she thinks you ought to entertain her."

"Well — can't we do something?" demanded Sally. "Four months — my goodness!"

"Why don't you and Jean talk to her? I don't answer her as much as you do. But she is sick — and it gets dull for her."

"We'll fix a schedule," suggested Jean. "Just so it won't make her worse."

"It might be good for her," said mother, her mind still on her counting. "We got off on the wrong foot, all of us feeling so sorry about the thing."

Sally was surprised how easy it was when you tried. She and Jean went in to see Betsy on Saturday morning, armed with a pad of paper and a pencil. They drew up an hourly schedule — certain times for reading aloud, certain hours for between-meal fruit juice and milk, mealtimes, naps, radio programs — no murders!

Ideas for passing the time suddenly sprouted into a dozen new devices. They listed an hour for special treats: each day after school one of them would bring a surprise home to Betsy. Twice a week she would get new library books. After supper every night, she could wear the precious watch for an hour. The hours of the day filled up astonishingly fast.

"Now," said Sally, looking over the chart, "this is the time for milk and graham crackers. Then in an hour it will be lunch. You get a library book for that hour. By the time you wake up from your nap we'll have a surprise ready. But the important thing is, don't ring your bell until four thirty this afternoon!"

"Why?" asked Betsy, her eyes sparkling at the mystery.

"Because it will interfere with something on this chart. If you don't call mother at the wrong time — or anyone else — you'll have a surprise for supper. See?"

After a conference with mother, they copied the chart in careful printing, and tacked it on the wall by Betsy's bed. For reference, copies were hung in the kitchen and in the girls' room. During the nap Sally and Jean shopped at the ten-cent store for a supply of surprises and rewards and prizes for the coming week.

By Sunday, Sally went to church with the satisfaction of a job well done. Betsy was occupied and happy all day long. In the afternoon Scotty stopped in, for the first time since Christmas, with a tiny potted plant for Betsy. Sally felt rewarded. In spite of Betsy's illness, a lot of nice things had happened since Christmas. Then she stopped in cold horror.

"Jean!" she cried. "How long is it since anyone looked at the Careys' house plants?"

JEAN clapped her hand over her mouth and goggled at Sally.

"I haven't thought of them since Betsy got sick," she said. "Have you?"

"Not since the day Dr. Neal was here." Sally counted on her fingers. Ten days. "How long can plants live without water?"

"I soaked them well the last time I was there," Jean remembered, "but that was the last — it was the Tuesday after school started. Two weeks ago!" She sagged back with a frown. Sally said faintly: "I was supposed to go the day Betsy got sick, and I forgot it then. Two weeks!"

Jean pulled herself out of her chair with a sigh. "It's only seven thirty. Let's go over and see the damages."

Mother sent Ricky along. She didn't like the idea of the girls going into an empty house after dark, but she admitted that they had better see about the plants as quickly as possible.

Sally found herself shivering as she thrust the key into the door. How could they ever replace that basket of ivy, trailing to the floor in the south window? And the wreath of philodendron around the sunroom windows — it would take years to grow another vine as long as that!

They thrust open the door and switched on the light

praying for a miracle. If a burglar had broken in, Sally felt quite sure that Mrs. Carey would have been happy to part with her silver tea set, as long as he happened to water the plants. They hurried through the living room, switching on lights as they went.

The ivy hung dry and brown. The philodendron was

yellow and withered. Jean nodded as if she'd known all along what to expect. Ricky let out a long whistle. "You've sure done it this time," he consoled the girls. Sticking his hands in his pockets, he strolled around to look for further damage. An African violet hung black and crumpled on the soil. The row of little red begonias on the kitchen window sill was completely dead.

Knowing what she would find, Sally turned toward the stairs. The philodendron around the lamp in the bedroom was gone. And the ivy trailing from a shelf in the bathroom. And a tall plant with speckled pointed leaves in the upper hall that she had always disliked.

Suddenly, feeling ashamed of herself, Sally had to giggle. The catastrophe was *so* complete. And the darn house was so full of plants!

Jean guffawed. Ricky began to snicker. The three of them sat down on the top step and laughed until the tears came. Finally Sally, wiping her eyes on her skirt, managed to calm down.

" Well, boys and girls," she said. " This is *it*. The complete and colossal failure. What do we do next? "

Ricky looked as if he knew just how they felt. " I'm glad it's your party, not mine," he said helpfully.

" How long have we got? " Sally asked.

" Mother said the middle of February," Jean remembered. " Well — do you see anything to resuscitate before we leave? "

" Not a thing," said Sally. " They're all ruined."

" Let's go home," said Ricky impatiently. " Looks to me like a case for mom."

" I'm afraid so," agreed Jean soberly. Sally hated to admit it, but in a crisis like this there was nothing to do but ask mother's advice.

" Are you sure you turned off every light? " mother asked at least three times, when she heard the story. They were sure of that, at least.

" Well — " mother sounded very serious. " Have you any plans? "

Sally glanced at her father. She knew what he would say, so she said it first. " Of course, we'll have to replace what we can. But what can we do about that enormous basket of ivy that she had for fifteen years? And the philodendron that trailed all around the windows? You can't *buy* plants like that — can you? "

"I never saw any," admitted mother. "But you can't let Mrs. Carey walk into her house and find things this way."

"All right," Sally saw the point. "I'll write her the bad news. I sure hate to tell her, though. She must have cherished that weedy old basket."

"Sally!" said her mother sharply. "There is no need to disparage her house and her tastes, just because you failed to take care of them. You'd better let me see the letter you write."

"O.K.!"

She and Jean went at once to the distasteful task.

"Couldn't we say they got a disease and died?" Sally asked hopefully, pausing at the turn of the stairs. "We could replace all the others, and —"

Dad looked up sharply. "If you want to tell a lie, make it a good one," he said sarcastically. "Tell her the house burned down and we got it rebuilt for her homecoming. Little lies are very thin."

Sally flushed. It wouldn't have been a lie, exactly, just to save face. Or would it? Sitting at the desk with the paper in front of her, she had to admit that it would have been.

"Dear Mrs. Carey," she began slowly, "I hate to tell you this, but we forgot your plants and they are all dead."

Reading over her shoulders, Jean giggled. "That's breaking it softly," she commented.

Sally tore up the page and began again.

"It's been an unusually busy winter, and Betsy is sick with rheumatic fever. When Jean and I went in to see your plants today, the big ivy was dead. I'm afraid the zero spell last week —"

"There wasn't any zero spell," objected Jean.

"How will she know?" retorted Sally. "She's in Florida."

"But people who go south in the winter always read the weather reports from back north. Don't think she won't know! Here, give me a piece of paper. I can do better than that."

After an hour's struggle, Sally took the letter down to her mother.

"Why don't you just say you don't know what to do about the big plants?" asked mother, handing back the note. "Maybe she will have a suggestion."

So the note was finally written, stating very simply that the girls were deeply sorry about their oversight, because they knew how much the plants had meant to Mrs. Carey, and they planned to replace what they could before she came home. But they didn't know what to do about the big ones.

Sally sealed and stamped the envelope with a somber realization that not only would there be no ten dollars from Mrs. Carey, but replacing the plants would cost another ten dollars, at least. It looked as if they would have to go on sitting for most of the spring. Two steps forward, and one step back. At that rate progress was slow indeed.

Trying to repair the damage took all day Saturday. The girls made an inventory of the plants in each container, threw out the dead ones, and then packed the containers in a market basket to take to the florist.

Over their lunch they consulted with mother about the list they had made. "How much do you suppose they will cost?" asked Sally as if she hated to hear the answer. Mother was jotting down figures and adding them up.

"About twelve dollars, I should think. Of course, that

will mean getting smaller plants than Mrs. Carey had too," she said. Sally and Jean looked at each other despondently.

"I've got fifty cents left this week," said Jean. "We'd better carry sandwiches again, Sally! If you'll give me next week's allowance today, mother — "

"That's only four-fifty, if you use it all," said Sally. "What would you use for bus fare? I've got a dollar, but — "

"I'll lend you ten dollars," said mother, at that point. "You can carry sandwiches and pay me back a couple of dollars a week — unless something else turns up."

"Like sitting," groaned Jean. "Only if we get into that again, we'll never get out."

"Stick to the sandwiches," advised mother comfortably. "It'll take only a month or so."

That afternoon they visited every florist shop in town before the plants were duplicated to their satisfaction. Mother went with them as they placed the plants about the house.

"You really wouldn't know the difference, would you?" said Sally wistfully. Mother was reassuring.

"You've done a good job, girls. They look as good as the originals."

But there was still the sunroom. After a look at that, mother said the only thing to do was to throw the big plants out. Actually the disappearance of the thick trailing vine around the windows modernized the room remarkably. On Sunday, Sally and Jean scrubbed the woodwork that had not been painted for years.

For the philodendron that had framed the window and the aged ivy there was still no solution. February was passing, and the girls were tense with the thought of the Careys' return.

Sally would have worried over Mrs. Carey more than she did, if it hadn't been for Betsy. Because she wasn't doing as well as she should, Dr. Neal was coming in to see her every other day. Sally met him on Friday as she came out from watering the plants a week after they had replaced them.

"How's Betsy, Dr. Neal?" she asked automatically, as he approached the sidewalk.

"Not so good, Sally," he said frankly. "I've been talking to your mother. You and Jean can help a lot. Betsy had better go to the hospital for some special care. But I think she's going to pull out of it all right."

Hospital! Sally stared after him, stunned with dismay, as he stepped briskly down to his car and drove off. She turned and fled into the house.

"Mother! I just saw Dr. Neal and he says —"

"Sh!" her mother held up a hand to stop her. "I don't want Betsy to hear until I can break it to her. He has detected a heart murmur, and he says hospital care is what she needs now. Dad and I are going up with her tonight."

Sally found herself shaking. None of the family had been in a hospital since Jimmy was born.

"But he — he says she'll pull out of it all right —"

Mother nodded, as if her thoughts were far away "Oh, yes, I know the hospital will take good care of her. Only — I hate to have her go. If we can just keep her from being homesick. Six weeks is such a long time."

Six weeks! Sally listened numbly, trying not to think of all the things she feared.

Betsy took the news more calmly than anyone else. She wanted to get well as soon as possible, and if that would happen more quickly in a hospital, she would make no fuss about going. When she found she was to

[149]

go in the ambulance, the whole trip became a dramatic adventure.

Sally was too restless to study while her parents were gone. Wandering into Betsy's room, she decided to put it in order. It was funny how empty the house seemed with Betsy gone. You thought you were crowded to the roof, but when one person in the family was missing, you simply rattled.

In fewer days than Sally would have dreamed possible, they were all used to the new routine of taking turns going to the hospital, and planning and sending little surprises and new books. At the end of the first week, Dr. Neal said the X-rays were encouraging, and that Betsy might be home for Easter.

Millie called the week before Valentine's Day to invite Sally to a party at her house.

"It's the first party I've had since I came back to Sherwood," she said. "Do say you can come. It's going to be loads of fun — and I'm having Eddie Lansing for you, and I want you to meet Joe Ballard. He's the man at King's department store, you know."

Sally accepted with cautious enthusiasm. She knew Millie would be really hurt if she didn't. And it would be fun to see Eddie Lansing again.

On Friday, Jimmy went off to school loaded with valentines for every member of his first-grade class. This was one of the biggest days of the year for him, and his chubby face shone with cheerful anticipation. When he came home that afternoon, he proudly counted out for his sisters the twenty-five valentines he had received, spreading them out on the rug to examine them all again.

Betsy's friend from the next block, who was in her room at school, brought home forty-one valentines for

Betsy, from everyone in her class, the teacher, the principal, and several of her friends in the other grades. Sally took them up to the hospital before supper and delivered a gilt-covered chocolate heart from her and Jean.

"Have fun while you can!" she said gaily. "Love was never like this in high school!"

Betsy, looking fine, was very happy in a ward with three other little girls. At least Sally didn't have to worry about her any more now. And she knew mother and dad believed Dr. Neal when he assured them she was coming along nicely. But they both looked pretty worn this week. Could it be the bills? There ought to be something she could do about it. But the dinner table wasn't the place to bring up such a problem; she'd try to talk to them later tonight.

And then she forgot about their worries entirely. Mother looked toward the window as they sat down at the table. "Why, I do believe the Careys are home!" she cried.

Sally's heart dropped with a dull thump, and she looked hastily at Jean. Ricky choked on his milk. "D Day," he muttered encouragingly.

"Should we go over tonight?" asked Sally, hoping her father would say no. Her mother considered a minute and said, "Not the minute they've come back." Sally's heart bounced up again in relief. "Tomorrow morning, I should think."

Sally got up early the next morning. Now that the hour of crisis was upon them, she wanted to get it over with. Promptly after breakfast, she and Jean turned their reluctant steps toward the Careys' front door and rang the bell.

"The worst she can do," she muttered to Jean, "is to

be terribly angry and scold for an hour. And maybe sever relations with the folks."

The door opened, and Mrs. Carey, regal and white-haired, brown-skinned from the Florida sun, smiled at them.

"Come in, girls. I thought you might be over."

Sally stole a sidewise glance at Jean, who was looking stoically ahead. Following Mrs. Carey into the sun-room, Sally thought critically that it looked better than it had with the vines trailing all over it. But of course Mrs. Carey had a right to her own opinion.

"I was terribly sorry to hear about Betsy," said Mrs. Carey, still friendly. "How is she getting along?"

"Just fine," said Jean, in a rather high voice. "She's used to the hospital now, and they seem to keep her busy. Dr. Neal says she's coming along very well."

"I'm delighted to hear that," said Mrs. Carey. "Tell her I shall go to see her soon. I have a collection of sea shells she might like to have."

Sally was beginning to relax and breathe more easily. She couldn't be mad at the whole family, then.

"I know she'd love them, Mrs. Carey," she said hastily, and then went on before she became tongue-tied. "We — uh, Jean and I — we just wanted to tell you how badly we feel about your plants. Really, we didn't forget them at all until Betsy got so sick — and then — "

Mrs. Carey grinned. Actually grinned. Then she laughed. Sally wondered, aghast, if the Florida sun had touched her mind.

"Well — we thought — " she began weakly. Mrs. Carey waved her hand toward the sunroom.

"You did a beautiful job of replacing things, girls," she said. "I think you showed a very mature sense of responsibility. As for the big ones — " she paused again

[152]

with a twinkle — "that big ivy in the box, and the philodendron around the windows, you'd never believe how
glad I am to see the last of them!" Sally stared at her,
and Jean's mouth fell open.

"But they were beautiful!" cried Sally, who had
never felt that way before.

"Oh, yes, in their way," nodded Mrs. Carey.
"They've been around here for fifteen years. Mother
started them from small plants, and they were her main
interest in life. When she died, five years ago, they were
left to me. And I can tell you I got tired of them. We
never could paint the woodwork under the vine, and
that ivy — I had to wash the leaves every week. I like
the small plants that I put around for a special reason —
not an overgrown forest like those!"

"But — but —" Sally almost stuttered in her confusion and curiosity, "why did you keep them all this
time, if you didn't like them?"

"Well — I just never had the heart to let them die,"
said Mrs. Carey frankly. "There they were, green and
healthy. But I can tell you it was a happy solution that
they were forgotten for a couple of weeks. And so un-
intentional! Now I can forget all about them and begin
housekeeping over again!"

Sally had to laugh, and Jean joined her. They giggled
happily and tearfully until Mrs. Carey rose.

"Now I want to settle what I owe you," she said,
groping in her black handbag.

"Oh, no, Mrs. Carey! Really, we couldn't take any
money. I mean, you don't owe us anything! Not after
letting everything die —" Sally was embarrassed to
death.

"Oh, yes, I do," said Mrs. Carey very definitely. "I
like your replacements as well as the originals — and you

[153]

had all the care of them. And as I told you, the other loss was a favor to me. So here is the ten dollars, and thank you very much!"

She put the bill in Sally's hand and snapped her purse shut.

"If you're going to do as well as this every time," she chuckled, "I'll hire you whenever we go out of town. At the very worst, it means new plants for me all around!" She went to the door with the girls, and cried after them, "Don't forget my message for Betsy!"

"Well!" said Sally inadequately, as they sagged down on their own living room couch. "What do you know about that?"

"People are nice," Jean agreed. "It just goes to show."

They delivered the bill to their mother, and totaled up their financial position. This unexpected adjustment put them in much better standing than they had feared. Sally calculated thankfully that she could manage now with her allowance. No more sitting after all!

Dizzy with relief, she thought of Millie's party. Now it could be a real celebration, and she felt just like one!

WHEN Millie first invited her, Sally had been dubious about going to a party with a crowd of people she hardly knew. But as Millie chattered on about her plans, the party began to sound exciting. Scotty would be there, although Millie explained that she really had to ask Louise because Scotty seemed to be going steady with her. But she was having Eddie Lansing for Sally, and, really, he was wonderful.

Mother looked unsettled when Sally told her about the plans. Sally knew she didn't think it was going to be the kind of party she wanted her daughter to go to, and yet how could she prove it? Finally she said, "Why, it sounds as if it ought to be fun."

Later she made an effort to find out more about it. "What are Millie's parties like, do you know?"

"No, I never went to one, and no one ever says anything, only —"

"Only?"

"What a wonderful time they had."

"Oh," remarked mother, as if that didn't mean much. "Well, did you say Scotty was going to be there?"

"That's what Millie said." Sally was trying not to be irritated, but she hated to discuss Millie when she knew mother was prejudiced.

"Of course, her folks will be there," mother said, a little uncertainly.

"But naturally!" said Sally. Who ever heard of giving a party without your parents' being somewhere around? Although it might be fun if you could get away with it!

Mother gave up then. Sally, with an uncomfortable feeling that mother might be right, half wished she weren't going. But there was no tactful way of getting out of it.

She decided to wear the rose-red crepe that she had worn to the football dance. And then she remembered that Eddie had met her in that dress. It would never do to let him suspect that she had only one date dress.

It was a difficult problem, but she finally chose her black crepe with gold belt and beads. Black was sophisticated, very appropriate for Eddie Lansing. She pinned back her hair with a pair of gold barrettes and slipped on a charm bracelet.

Satisfied, she tripped downstairs. Since Millie's house was only three doors down the street, she was going to meet Eddie there.

"Don't be too late," her father said, as usual.

"O dad!" Sally exclaimed in protest. "I'll be home when the party is over. My goodness!"

"Well, 'be good, sweet maid, and let who will be clever,'" he cautioned her. She closed the door with a small slam that might have been accidental. Really! Father said that almost every time she went out, and it wasn't funny at all.

As she approached the Davis house, she saw Millie's parents going out to their car. So they weren't going to be home after all! But maybe it was just an early movie. She turned in and rang the bell.

"Sally!" Millie was extra-cordial, in a swishing red dress that looked very glamorous. "You look simply wonderful! Come on downstairs. I'm dying for you to meet Joe Ballard."

"I saw your folks going out," said Sally, and then she wished she hadn't. Millie's face looked a little hard, and she said, with a touch of bitterness: "Oh, sure, they have a party of their own! They couldn't stay around for mine! But it's no loss. We'll have fun."

Sally followed her downstairs doubtfully. And then she relaxed. After all, she couldn't turn around and go home. And the gaily decorated room was very inviting. Paper hearts hung from ribbons tacked to the ceiling. A dart board on the far wall was outlined with a huge paper heart, and the darts had been stuck through small hearts.

Joe Ballard met them at the foot of the steps. He was older than the high-school crowd — about twenty, perhaps — with a half-grown crew cut and a look of being crowded into civilian clothes. It was plain that he thought Millie was fascinating.

"Sally, this is Joe," Millie said, with an air of pride. Joe smiled and shook hands with Sally. But his eyes were for Millie.

"Come over here." Millie seized her hand and dragged her over to a corner. "I want you and Eddie Lansing to get acquainted. You're both kind of special people."

Eddie pulled himself to his feet, dark and slender and smooth, a sophisticated expression on his narrow face.

"We already know each other," he told Sally, with a smile meant for her alone. "We danced together last Thanksgiving. How could I forget?"

"Of course you couldn't," Sally told him, astonished at her own response. She smiled up at him, and Millie and Joe wandered away as he took her hand and said: " Shall we dance again? Why wait? "

" I'd love to," said Sally as he led her over to the record player.

" Smooth or hot? " He held a record behind his back as if he were sure of her answer.

" Oh, smooth! " said Sally.

" I knew it! "

No one had ever made dancing mean so much before. Sally was in heaven. By the second dance she wondered if she could be falling in love. She'd never felt like this about Scotty, for all her anguish over him.

Once, looking over Eddie's shoulder, her eyes met Scotty's. He and Louise had come in during the dance and he seemed to be observing Sally's partner sharply. Then Louise whispered something that he had to bend his head to hear and they began to dance too, Louise clinging and flattering, acting as if Scotty were the only man in the room. Sally could see it without annoyance. She should care!

At the end of the record, Scotty stood beside them. He shook hands rather belligerently with Eddie, and asked Sally if she wanted to trade a dance. Without giving her a chance to speak, Eddie gathered Sally into his arms and moved away to the music, saying, " Not yet, sonny, she's got this one booked."

Sally smiled up at him, trying to sound as sophisticated as he was, and said lightly, " Is this a monopoly? "

" Would you mind? " he whispered, tightening his arm.

By ten o'clock the dancing stopped for games. The boys threw darts while the girls formed a cheering section. Then Louise introduced an intricate game of forfeits, and for the first time some of the glow went out of

[158]

the evening. The forfeits were kisses, and Sally cringed a little. Kissing games were exciting if you didn't get caught. But she had a fastidious prejudice against kissing just anyone. Even Eddie, she thought, facing reality coldly.

Luck was with her, and she managed to escape a forfeit, although she sensed that Eddie was wondering why. Somewhere before the game ended Scotty had managed to pull out of it and was throwing darts by himself in the corner.

After that the party began to get a little rowdy.

"Cigarette?" Eddie Lansing was at her elbow.

"No, thank you," Sally declined, without even trying to be mysterious about it.

"Dance?" The cigarette in his mouth was half gone, and he put it out. Scotty, with Louise at his elbow, was starting the record machine again. Only two other couples joined them this time, and even Eddie seemed to be dancing more to pass the time than because he preferred to. It was after eleven. The food should be coming along pretty soon.

"What this party needs now is a couple of highballs," said Bud Clayton, a weedy youth with an unhealthy complexion. Millie giggled up at him brightly.

"Is that the answer?" she laughed. "Dad's supply is right under the bar over there." No one was dancing now, but Scotty went on putting a record on the player. Bud Clayton lounged behind the bar. "What'll you have, folks?"

Hoping for some support, Sally looked up at Eddie. But she knew she was going to be alone in this crowd. "Make it a rum coke, sugar," he murmured. "That's what I'm having."

"Make mine plain ginger ale," said Sally firmly. He

cocked an eyebrow mockingly. " Sure? "

" Sure! "

Scotty and Louise came over.

" Sally, what do you think? " cried Louise in a tone of mocking complaint. " Scotty says he's strong enough to finish the evening on ginger ale! " She clung to his arm and looked up at him teasingly. " The big boss doesn't think this little girl ought to have any fun! "

Scotty looked bored. " O.K., it's your recipe," he said indifferently. " Want some ginger ale, Sally? "

" Thanks, Eddie is bringing mine," said Sally demurely. So Scotty was keeping an eye on her manners, was he? Louise looked at Sally with an amused gesture of intimacy while Scotty stood at the bar.

" Men! " she said, with a small laugh. " Eddie looks pretty smooth, Sally. Scotty ought to get over being so touchy."

" He *is* smooth," Sally told her. Eddie brought over a frosted glass and took Sally's elbow intimately.

" Let's have a little private conversation," he murmured, as he steered her toward the couch in the corner. All the early glow had faded, and Sally was beginning to be wary. She sat in the middle of the couch, ignoring his signals to move a little closer, and lifted her glass to her lips. It didn't smell like ginger ale. She sniffed again, and didn't like it. Eddie took a long drink and set his glass down on the floor. His face was flushed now and his eyes were openly eager.

" You are the cutest trick I've turned up in my high-school career," he murmured. " I wanta see lots of you, baby."

His head was almost on her shoulder, and Sally edged back. This was getting sticky. " It's a nice party," she babbled, pretending to sip her drink, and gagging at the scent. "Have you known Millie long?"

"Not as long as I'm going to know you, sweetie-pie. I never thought I'd find a girl who could dance like that."

He moved closer as she edged away, so tense she was almost shaking. She saw Scotty dealing out a hand of solitaire and looking her way from time to time. Sally thought of Louise.

"You're pretty smooth on the dance floor yourself," she said, trying desperately to keep him talking. "Can we have another? There's a girl here who's simply struck with you."

He raised his head and peered around the room.

"Only one I want struck with me," he said.

Someone was turning the lights low. Sally set her glass on the floor, hoping someone would knock it over. She had to get out of this some way.

"Look," she said, jumping to her feet so suddenly that Eddie lurched before he could recover himself, "there's the clock striking twelve. I've got to go. I have to be in —"

She felt as if she were babbling pointlessly, but to her immense relief Scotty was beside her.

"We've got a dance before the party breaks up," he said quietly. Thankfully she went into his arms, feeling as if she were escaping from a nightmare. He danced her toward the door without any words. Over his shoulder she could see Eddie looking after them foggily and then turning to Louise, who was standing near him.

"This will go on for hours yet," Scotty muttered. "I've had enough. What about you?"

"Oh, let's get out of here!" breathed Sally. They slipped out of the room, found their coats, and made their way up to the front door. Behind them they could hear the record end, the needle scratching round and round, until someone yelled, "Turn off the music, for cat's sake!"

Out in the cold February night, with the clean stars sharp in the black sky, Sally's cheeks felt hot and flushed. She trudged along with her hands in her pockets and her head down. Scotty walked beside her, whistling under his breath.

"Thanks," she said, at her door. "I couldn't have stood it much longer. It was nice of you to pull me out."

"That's O.K.," he tossed off the evening. "I didn't think much of it myself. They're out of our league, that gang."

He turned away as casually as he ever had. Sally was about to say something, but she caught it back. Never let him think she was trying to keep him with her!

At the edge of the steps he turned again.

"So long, kid!" he said, and, as an afterthought, "Be seeing you!"

CHAPTER
SIXTEEN

WHEN Sally woke up Sunday morning after the party, the memory was like ashes in her mouth. That awful Eddie Lansing! She didn't see now how she could ever have thought he was attractive. Thank goodness she was through with him!

Then she remembered Scotty. He had been concerned about her. He had rescued her from a sordid situation and brought her home. He was simply wonderful! For a hazy moment she shut her eyes and dreamed.

She opened her eyes again and cut off the dream before it got out of control. Scotty had been sweet. But he just felt big-brotherly because she was the little girl down the block. Better think about something else, anything different. Operetta, for instance. Tryouts were coming this week. But what good would it do? The New Year wasn't turning out as well as it had looked on January first!

She writhed when she thought of Millie. Mother might not say, " I thought as much," but the implication would be there. Jean would look as if anyone but a nitwit would have known what would happen. Maybe she wouldn't have to see so much of Millie, now that the girl had Joe. With a gesture of exasperation, Sally threw the covers back and jumped out of bed. The important thing was not to let on to the family. She certainly didn't want to have to talk about it!

"Did you have a good time?" Mother looked up from the paper as Sally came into the dining room. Sally busied herself with orange juice and a sweet roll, standing by the sideboard as she gulped down the juice. Then she went out into the kitchen to see what was hot. She had planned this conversation as she dressed. Don't say too much or too little. Be as casual as possible.

"Not very," she said, coming back into the dining room with a plate of scrambled eggs.

"Oh?" Mother was interested.

"It was a different crowd from the kids I know," Sally was trying not to speak too rapidly, "and — oh, I don't know — it just wasn't as much fun as our parties."

She had an uncomfortable feeling that mother was reading the whole story behind her vague words. But, mother, who could be very tactful when she wanted to be, returned to her paper and said no more. Jean looked interested, but received no encouragement. Sally picked up the funny paper and hid behind it.

Scotty wasn't at church this morning. That was odd. He almost never missed a Sunday. When the service was over, Sally felt better about last night. But she came home feeling vaguely disappointed in not seeing Scotty there.

He wasn't at the young people's meeting either. Afterward they had fun with a treasure hunt — looking for a Willkie button, an alderman's signature, a pretzel, a stamp canceled in 1945. But Sally drew Bob Cornell for a partner, a thickset blond junior, with nothing to talk about except winning the hunt. It was only by stern self-discipline that she kept herself from telling him outright that she thought treasure hunts were silly.

Afterward she came home early, alone. Jean had gone to someone's house with Jeff. But no one had asked Sally tonight — not that she cared. Only it was depressing to walk home alone. She looked down the block toward Scotty's house. There were lights all over the house. Instantly she worried — was Scotty sick? That would account for his not being at St. Paul's this morning or this evening.

Mother and dad were in the living room when she came in, listening to a symphony, while mother mended socks.

"Did you hear about Mrs. Scott's heart attack?" mother asked as Sally came in.

"No! I didn't know there was anything wrong with her heart!"

Mother looked serious and a little excited, the way she got about neighborhood crises. "It happened this morning. She's had some kind of trouble, high blood pressure, or something, for years. Dr. Neal stopped in this evening to talk about Betsy, and he told us then. She's getting along all right now, but she'll have to take things very easy for quite a while."

So that was why Scotty hadn't been around! It gave Sally quite a turn. Scotty's mother! Why, it could be her own mother. Mrs. Scott wasn't so old.

"You haven't got high blood pressure or anything, have you?" she demanded, worried.

"Not me!" mother reassured her comfortably. "You don't need to worry." The slight smile around her eyes showed that she was pleased with Sally's concern. Then she remembered something else.

"Have you heard from Conover yet?"

"No," said Sally shortly. She was beginning to feel sensitive on the subject of college.

[165]

"That's all right, then," said mother, snipping a thread, and rolling two socks into a ball.

"Why?" Sally asked. "Do you think — don't you think — ?"

"I don't think we can send you away next year after all."

Sally stared from her mother to her father. He seemed to be listening to the conversation attentively, not ready to talk yet.

"But, mother, surely I can go somewhere!" she cried. "Conover isn't the only place — I'd just as soon go to Western State — my grades are good enough —"

Her mother laid down the darning ball, and gestured to Sally to sit down. "It isn't your grades," she said gently. "It's just that with all Betsy's illness is going to cost now, there isn't going to be any money."

"But, mother," said Sally on a deep breath of protest, "what on earth would I do?"

Dad looked ironic, as he did when he invited his supposedly intelligent children to look the facts of life in the face.

"You can get a perfectly good education right here at Northern University," he suggested, as if it were too obvious to need saying.

"Northern!" Sally repeated in a whisper. Everyone she knew was going away. There wouldn't be anyone left in town. It was the one tragedy she had thought wouldn't happen to her.

"The bills for Betsy are going to run close to fifteen hundred dollars," said mother, as if she'd been thinking about it quite a bit.

Dad looked over and said peremptorily: "Now, Sara, quit worrying! I told you the money was in the bank for Betsy. I'll just get to work this summer and finish that history of English literature I've had on the fire. When that's published, we'll be in the clear again."

Sally knew about that history. Dad had been working on it for years, pouring his life's blood into his work. It was to be his masterpiece. How could he just get to work and finish it up this summer? Mother looked as if she felt the same way, and suddenly Sally felt as if she just couldn't bear it, to have mother and dad, who were such sturdy supports, worried and hurt on her account.

"That's all right," she said hurriedly. "I'll get a job or something. I don't have to go to college."

Mother looked at dad, and dad cocked an eyebrow, meaning: She doesn't know what she's saying. She'll get over it.

"O.K.," said Sally, getting up. "Was that all you wanted to say? I'll figure something out."

She climbed the stairs, feeling tired out. Everything happened to her. Here was this dismal last year at high school, and now she couldn't look forward to anything next year either. Nobody liked her but people like Millie and Eddie. And Al Carter, who still called about once a month. She'd counted so much on getting away next year!

Downstairs a door banged, and Jean blew in. Jean was just beginning to have fun, Sally thought, with a sigh for her own hard lot. For Sally, life was practically over.

Jean bounced up the stairs, whistling very accurately, "We're called gondolieri," and breezed in, breaking into trills as she opened the door.

"You know, Jeff is kind of cute," she said. "He was terribly smart about the treasure hunt. And then we all went over to his house for food, and he plays the piano too, and we sang —" She began to undress. Sally sat

[167]

morosely at her desk, wondering how anyone could feel so good. Jean whistled another bar, and broke off again.

"Are you going to try out for the operetta this week?" she demanded.

"I don't know," said Sally listlessly. "What's the use?"

The high school was putting on *The Gondoliers* this year, and the tryouts were immediately ahead. Jean had been practicing the songs ever since tryouts had been announced.

"Well, it's going to be a very cute show," said Jean positively. "You'll be a dope if you don't at least make a try for it. There's nothing wrong with your voice. You ought to make the chorus at least."

"Well—" Sally jabbed at her memo pad with her pencil.

"They say that Scotty has a good voice," reported Jean casually.

"Oh?" Maybe it wouldn't be a bad idea to try out. "Did you hear about his mother?"

Jean nodded. "She's going to be all right, I guess. Anyway, I wouldn't be surprised if he were a lead. It's hard to find a boy with any voice at all."

Sally wouldn't have admitted even to herself that Jean's report decided her. But it did seem stupid not to try out for one of the biggest events of the year. Trying to sound as if it really were unimportant, she said, "Do you want to run over some of the songs with me tomorrow night?"

"Sure," said Jean, with equal indifference. "Chorus tryouts don't begin until Wednesday."

She went to sleep wondering about Mrs. Scott. Could she phone Scotty to say she was sorry about his mother, or would that look as if she just wanted an excuse to call him? And if she didn't, would he think she didn't care? It was a difficult problem. She finally decided to call him Monday night.

Then she didn't have to after all. He was on the same bus, coming home that afternoon, and as they got off together, she said, "I was terribly sorry to hear about your mother, Scotty."

He nodded. "It was kind of tough, all right. But the doctor says there's nothing to worry about, if she doesn't get upset." He looked uneasy as he said it, and Sally wanted to comfort him. But there wasn't much she could do.

To her surprise, he stopped at her walk a minute.

"I gotta hurry home," he explained. "Someday I'll come in for some food. But mom likes to see me. She oughta be up by next week."

Sally watched him for a minute, as he strode down the block, his head slightly thrown back, his whistle falling on the air. He was sweet. She hoped his mother's illness wouldn't keep him from the operetta work.

Rumors about the leads were flying all week. Millie was reputed to have a surprisingly good voice. Sylvia Decker was another. What do you know about Scotty's being a singer? Wouldn't it be a scream if Louise turned out to be the opposite number?

The cast, with understudies for all the leads, was to be posted on the music bulletin board by three o'clock Friday. By that day Sally found herself eager to know the results.

On her way to the music room after her last class, she ran into Millie. Sally hadn't seen her since her party, nor even talked to her, which was unusual.

"That was a nice party," Sally told Millie, feeling guilty about leaving without saying farewell to her hostess.

"Quite a brawl," agreed Millie complacently. "Say, what happened to you? We were having food about one o'clock, and Eddie was looking all over for you!"

Sally felt a revulsion of distaste at the memory.

"I wasn't feeling well," she tried to make it convincing, "and Eddie was dancing with Louise, so Scotty took me home."

"Eddie is quite a boy, isn't he? He thinks you're wonderful," Millie chattered on. "He's going to call you for a date any minute. I told him you couldn't go out week nights, and he said for you he'd even wait until Saturday. You really went over with him!"

"That's nice," said Sally, shuddering inwardly. "I was surprised — I mean, he seemed so, well, so sort of experienced and everything. I didn't think I was his type."

Millie nodded sagely.

"He thought you were different. 'Slick chick,' he said. That's something, from Eddie."

With relief, Sally edged up to the crowd about the music bulletin board. The next moment she saw with horror that Eddie Lansing was there too.

"Hi, Eddie!" Millie cried before Sally could stop her. He turned and smiled, that knowing smile that Sally detested. But he acted very casual, said hello as if he had seen her somewhere once, and then, as the girls approached the board, he backed away and left.

Sally heaved a sigh of relief. Undoubtedly Millie had made a mistake about Eddie. She loved to think someone was mad about somebody else, and she could be so

[170]

wrong. Sally put Eddie out of her mind and turned to read the list.

Scotty was going to be Marco, for goodness' sake! And Louise would be Gianetta, Marco's bride. Sally felt a depressing foreboding. It wouldn't be so much fun to see Scotty playing opposite Louise every rehearsal! What made her think she wanted to be in this thing?

Millie was Casilda. That was all right. She'd be pretty in the part. Most of the other leads were people she knew so slightly that she didn't care at all. Sally was in the chorus, all right. So was Jean. And Jeff Sutton. And Eddie. Now she was sure it wouldn't be fun.

"I think I'm going to like this," Millie was murmuring in her ear. "That lead opposite me is terribly cute. Don't you know him? Only, of course, now that I'm going with Joe, I don't notice anyone else. At least, hardly ever."

"Mm —" Sally wasn't listening. "Let's get along, shall we? I promised Betsy I'd stop in at the hospital today on the way home and tell her about the operetta."

"Want to do something tonight?" Millie asked, just before Sally left the bus at the hospital stop. Sally spoke over her shoulder, standing at the door. "I can't make it tonight, Millie," she said as she swung off.

There was a letter from Conover when she got home. Sally tore it open with shaking fingers. If they rejected her application now, it wouldn't matter. If they didn't — she read the page in a tumult of confusion.

Dear Miss Burnaby:
   Although our enrollments have been closed since Thanksgiving, owing to some recent cancellations, we are pleased to inform you that we are able to accept your application at this date. Please

[171]

send us the matriculation fee, with the enclosed forms, upon receipt of which you will be assigned your quarters for next year.

Yours truly,

Estelle Baily, Registrar.

Sally clutched the letter, breathing fast and reading it over and over. Before, knowing she couldn't go away hadn't mattered quite so much. But here was the official acceptance. Surely something could be done: she could sit all year, she could work all summer, she could borrow the money.

She smoothed the letter out and reread it for the fourth time, and thought of Betsy whom she had just left. Fifteen hundred dollars. She couldn't earn that quickly! She thought of mother's worry and dad's book that he was going to rush faster than he'd wanted to, and all the money Jean needed for allowance and clothes and dues. And Ricky. Five children. Even if she earned part of her way, it would be hard on everyone.

With a glance at her watch, she ran upstairs. There would be just time before dinner to write her own cancellation. Get it over with before it hurt more than it did now.

CHAPTER
SEVENTEEN

SALLY felt a little guilty about turning Millie down so brusquely, but she had decided that, even though her social life was pretty empty these days, the less she saw of Millie the better.

She was considering the prospect of a dateless week end when the telephone rang. Hopefully she picked it up.

"Hello? Oh, hello." The letdown sound of the second hello made Jean raise her head with a grin: "No, I can't go tomorrow. No, I'm going to be busy. Thanks just the same."

Banging down the receiver, she turned to Jean with flaming cheeks. "Eddie Lansing! Ick! I wouldn't go out with him if he were the last boy in the school!"

"Is he so terrible?" asked Jean interestedly. "I thought he looked kind of sophisticated and hard to get."

"You should know!" said Sally darkly. Jean looked expectant. Almost without intending to, Sally found herself telling Jean the details about Millie's party. "Now, don't ever mention it to mother," she warned her sister over and over. "She'd be frantic and she'd worry — and after all, it's over now. Goodness knows, I'll see that I don't get into a spot like that again. But she'd tell me not to, anyway."

Jean was filing her nails with long, hasty strokes.

"Mother is always giving us advice," she agreed, "but at least by now we know what to do and Millie doesn't. It's more comfortable the Burnaby way than the Davis way."

"Oh, yes," Sally nodded emphatically. "I wouldn't have parents like Millie's for anything. Not for anything! But sometimes I wish mother wouldn't tell me not to do the things I wouldn't do anyway."

"Well, yes," said Jean, as if she knew what Sally meant.

In spite of her intense dislike for Eddie, Sally couldn't help noticing his popularity at the operetta rehearsals. Lots of the other girls seemed delighted to sit with him and exchange jokes, and he always took a crowd home in his car afterward. But for Sally he had only the slightest nod. Sometimes he didn't notice her at all.

That should have been entirely satisfactory, in the light of Sally's feelings toward him. But it wasn't. After a week and a half of his indifference, she couldn't help wondering about Millie's report on the state of his heart. Apparently he was easily discouraged. And, possibly he hadn't been entirely to blame for his actions on Valentine's night. If the Davises had been home, he wouldn't have acted like that. He could be charming if he were to improve, or even reform.

It was a stimulating thought. Inspiring a reform would be a gratifying experience. Perhaps he really cared for her, underneath, but was too hurt to show his feelings. If he did, why, then he ought to do whatever she asked. Just being friendly with him wouldn't do any harm.

In spite of his friendliness with the other girls, Sally had no difficulty in letting Eddie know that she had changed her mind. She smiled at him openly and began to get those twittery sensations when he looked straight at her. She thought she could read in his eyes heartbreak over his repulse and awakening hope.

Watching Scotty and Louise wasn't as hard as she had expected. The tone of the whole operetta was so gay and amusing, the love-making so farcical, that there could never be any question that Scotty was acting a part, and doing it well. In between their time on the stage, he and Louise were almost never together. He too was busy with lots of other girls. But after every rehearsal he filled his car with boys and girls going his way, and Sally and Jean were always included.

One night, two weeks after rehearsals had started, Sally was almost sure that Eddie was going to ask her to ride home with his crowd, when Scotty appeared at her elbow with his casual, "Ride home, Burnabys?" and she found that Eddie had moved on.

If he'd call for a date now, Sally thought, lingering a little to watch him, she'd rather like to go out with him. She had plans for his future that would be good for him.

During the last week of rehearsal the cast began working nights. The first performance was scheduled for Friday evening. Monday and Tuesday were careful, full-scale rehearsals, with the orchestra and lights and timing. Wednesday would be the dress rehearsal. Thursday the entire cast was to go to bed early to be fresh and rested for the opening performance.

On Monday night Eddie sat beside Sally whenever he was off stage. His behavior was very gentlemanly, and when Marco sang, "Take a pair of sparkling eyes," he hummed it through for Sally and said, with a quick glance and a smile: "'Take and keep them if you can!' My favorite song in the whole show!"

When the rehearsal was ended, he caught her hand in the confusion backstage, and said, "Say, we ought to celebrate Wednesday night!"

"That's a wonderful idea!" Sally told him, feeling that the high point of the operetta had been achieved.

"O.K. — I'll tell the crowd." Sally didn't particularly want the crowd. But bringing Eddie around to her way of thinking would have to be a gradual process; she couldn't do it the first time she went out with him.

On Tuesday the performance was wonderful. Everyone was in perfect voice; the choruses had never sung so well. Scotty was outstanding. By ten thirty the cast felt on top of the world, as they began to collect their wraps.

"Dress rehearsal will probably be terrible," said Millie, as if she knew all about those things. "They say it always is."

Eddie was beside Sally, and she smiled at him with a special twinkle. He held her shoulders in both hands, as he whispered in her ear.

"Why don't we celebrate tonight?" he suggested. "This is the time we feel like it. By tomorrow we'll probably be too depressed to care." He glanced over toward Millie. "Tell the gang we're going someplace."

"Swell!" cried Millie. "I'm just in the mood!"

For once, Sally agreed with her. She glanced at Eddie from under her lashes and he squeezed her elbow. "Are you with me?"

"Yes," she said happily. Everything was working out right, Sally thought as she found her coat. Tonight was just the beginning. She would let him know how disappointed she had been in his drinking at Millie's party, and he would give it up -- for her.

Scotty came by, in his usual manner. "Going home,

Burnabys? Come on." And for once his easygoing indifference was shaken, when Sally said happily: " I'm going with Eddie tonight, thanks just the same. Tell Jean to tell the folks."

" Jean's gone with Jeff," said Scotty.

" O.K., I'll call them," said Sally lightly. She was pleased to have him realize that she didn't have to rely on him.

They piled into the car — Ann Tweedy and Dick Hodges and Ken Rickett in back, Sally and Millie in front.

" Where are we going? " Millie leaned forward to ask Eddie.

" The Ranch House? Let's." Sally looked up at Eddie, certain that he would agree with whatever she suggested. But, instead, he turned slightly toward the three in the back seat and asked, " Where to, gang? "

There was a small scuffle in the back seat, and Ken Rickett said: " Ann is making a noise about not being late. But she'll go along with us, won't you, Annie? "

Ann giggled. " You boys are just awful. Really, Ken, I can't be out late."

" Make it Angelo's," called Dick Hodges. " We'll get the girls home by eleven. O.K.? "

" Well," Ann was letting herself be persuaded with a show of reluctance. Sally was frozen with dismay. As the car turned west from the driveway out of the school lot, she turned to Eddie.

" Eddie, I don't want to go to Angelo's. Honestly, I mean it! Besides, I have to call the folks as soon as we stop. Can't we make it the Ranch House? "

" You'll like Angelo's," Eddie assured her. " We're all pooped after that drill, and a little drink is what we want to fix us up for tomorrow. Look, if we get you home at

[177]

eleven, your folks aren't going to kick, are they? You can tell them rehearsal was late — "

"You can tell them we all went to the Ranch House," Millie suggested plausibly. "You know some of the others went there."

"Well, why don't we?" demanded Sally angrily. Eddie grinned at her masterfully.

"The Ranch House doesn't have the kind of drinks we want, beautiful," he said.

All at once it came over her what a mistake she had made. She should have known better. An uncomfortable inner voice whispered that she had got herself into this, but she told herself it was all Eddie's fault. Now she really did hate him!

Angelo's was a little shack five miles west of town on a side road, where, it was rumored, high-school students could be served liquor. The car picked up speed. Inside of ten minutes they were parked.

Sally sat sulkily as the others climbed out. She was about to announce that she would wait in the car, when she realized how alone she would be there, and how unsavory the surroundings were. In cold anger she got out too, and entered the dim, smoky bar.

"O.K., folks, here we are!" Eddie led them to a table, and they sat down, the other two boys noisy and gay. Millie was sparkling, and Ann seemed to be enjoying herself, in spite of her earlier qualms. No one paid any attention to Sally's stormy resistance.

"Make mine a beer," said Ken and Dick in unison. "Beer for me," said Millie, in a high voice. "I don't like beer," protested Ann. "Rum coke," suggested Ken, and she accepted that.

"I'll have a ginger ale," said Sally tightly.

"Oh, come on, Sally," said Eddie, "you're among

friends. Don't spoil the party."

"Beer is harmless," Millie assured her.

"Ginger ale." Sally was obstinate.

"O.K." Eddie gave the order to the waiter, and added the ginger ale with a wink, which Sally detected.

"If you put anything in it," she said quickly to the waiter, "I'll pour it on the floor right here."

The waiter, a cynical little Italian, suddenly softened.

"You'll get it straight, sister," he assured her.

The drinks were a long time coming, and Sally grew more uneasy by the minute. This was the worst jam she had ever been in. She sat silent and unhappy while the others sipped their beer, joking in double talk and screaming with laughter. Sally grew increasingly aware of the glances thrown their way by adult patrons.

It seemed forever until the boys finished their glasses. Millie and Ann were smoking their second cigarettes, when Eddie signaled the waiter to reorder. Sally came out of herself in time to realize what he was doing.

"Listen," she said, tensely determined, "we're going now. And I mean *now!* If not, I'm calling the folks this minute to come out and get me."

She turned to the waiter. "Where is the telephone?"

He was uneasy, knowing well enough what it would mean for Angelo, if angry parents invaded the place. But Ann looked at her watch with a squeak of alarm and came over to Sally's support.

"Oh, I've got to go too! It's going on twelve! I don't know what mother will say!" She began to gather things together, and Sally left her chair and walked to the door. Millie looked disappointed, but followed the girls, and the boys gave up the battle.

"All right, sourpuss," said Eddie vindictively. "You

[179]

wanted to get home fast. Here we go."

And they went. Sally gripped her hands together and pressed her feet against the floor, praying all the way that they would get home without an accident. She shut her eyes, but at one close call, when the sudden stop almost threw her against the windshield, she decided it would be safer to see what was happening. The ride was even worse than the roadhouse, she thought, clenching her teeth until her jaws ached. Eddie picked up speed again. He had determined to pass a transcontinental moving van lumbering along ahead at fifty miles an hour.

" Don't! " Sally implored him, breaking her intention not to speak to him again. " It's suicide. Don't, Eddie! "

He threw her a malicious smile, as he pressed the accelerator and shot ahead. " You said fast, sister. This is it! "

Sally shut her eyes again, praying with all the faith she had that she would get home. In those few seconds she almost grew up. It was her own fault she was in this spot.

The back seat was silent. So was Millie. Sally opened her eyes a minute. Millie was looking a little tense. Just a little. The three in back looked as if it were a point of honor not to express fear, but they were tense too. The moving van was behind them. For the moment they were safe.

Sally drew a deep breath. She knew what to do now.

"Nice going, Eddie," she said, making the compliment sincere. "You sure know how to drive. But when I said fast, I didn't mean *quite* that fast. Can't we relax for the last couple of miles and enjoy the night?"

"Can we?" Eddie looked at her suspiciously and she smiled brightly. He slackened the speed down to fifty, and some of the tension left his face.

"You could be such a cute kid," he muttered, "if you'd just *give* a little and not be so darned superior!"

He paid attention to his driving then, and Sally thought about his words. He had been trying to make her over in his pattern. Why should she hold that against him? She almost giggled, as she thought of the plans she'd had along the same lines. Who was she to change him?

In front of the house, Eddie got out of the car and stood there for a minute.

"Good night, Eddie," said Sally, knowing it was good-by for good. "I'm sorry I spoiled your party. Honestly."

She smiled as she said it, and he took her hand.

"We'll try it again sometime," he promised with a

flash of teeth. "It could have been fun!"

The car drove away and Sally dragged herself slowly into the house. Now that the evening was over, the letdown was exhausting, and she still had to face her family.

CHAPTER EIGHTEEN

THE lights were on in the living room. And on the porch. Of course, dad and mother were waiting up. Sally had known they would be. She could feel the tension in the air as she fumbled with her key.

"*Where* have you been?" asked mother, the moment Sally came into the house. Dad was pacing the floor. Actually pacing! Mixed with her nervousness and apprehension Sally felt a sense of irritation rise within her. *Why* didn't they wait for her explanation? Why couldn't they see her side of the story for once?

Mother looked too upset to see it anybody's way but her own. And for the first time in her life Sally had a glimmer of someone else's point of view. They had really been scared.

"Well, after rehearsal we all felt so good we thought we'd get something to eat — to celebrate. Eddie Lansing asked me to go with his gang. Millie was with us too."

"Millie again! Ha!" That was dad's opinion of Millie.

"And Ann Tweedy and Dick Hodges and Ken Rickett. I thought I could call you, but there wasn't any phone, and we didn't think we'd be so late. But —"

"Late! I should think you were! I've got a good no-tion to keep you out of the operetta! Who is this Eddie Lansing? He hasn't been around, has he?" Dad was thoroughly angry.

"No. I met him at Millie's party." Sally wished she didn't sound so guilty. But she couldn't say any more without telling too much.

Mother was staring at her oddly. Dad looked baffled.

"I don't know why you couldn't call. Wasn't there a telephone?"

Sally felt trapped. She simply couldn't let them know where she'd been. "I just couldn't," she said helplessly. "And we thought we were going to go home any minute."

Dad threw out his hands in disgust. "You're as bad as Ricky! Didn't it ever occur to you that we'd worry? Scotty came home an hour and a half ago. What were we to think?"

Sally was silent. Couldn't parents ever understand why you did things sometimes? And that you wished you hadn't?

Mother said wearily: "It's too late to talk about it any more now. Get to bed, Sally, and don't disturb Jean. We'll have to have an understanding about tomorrow night."

Dad snorted. "I'll come and get you myself, if I have to."

"O dad, no!" That would be the ultimate humiliation, to have a father call for a senior after rehearsal!

"Well, we'll see," said her father dubiously. "If I thought you'd come home with Scotty, I wouldn't worry. And stay away from this Eddie. He doesn't sound good to me."

"O.K." Sally climbed the stairs, feeling as if she'd been beaten. It had been ten years since dad had talked

to her like that. And telling her to see no more of Eddie!
As if she had to be told!

She undressed in the dark, and minute by minute her
anger slipped away. Parents might be difficult at times
like this, but maybe they had a reason. It did make it
a little easier to know for sure what you were expected
to do. As she fell asleep, a small, comforting realization
lightened her thoughts. Mother had seemed to know,
even without saying anything, how these things could
happen.

To her astonishment, Scotty joined her on the way
to the bus in the morning. That hadn't happened all
year. He was waiting for her on the sidewalk when she
came out of the house.

"Have fun last night?" he asked. Sally watched her
stadium boots scuffing chips of dried snow along the
walk.

"Not much," she said, shifting her load of books onto
one arm.

"I didn't think you liked that bunch," Scotty sounded
sulky, and Sally glanced up. His mouth was straight
and he looked a little bitter. Could he possibly have
been offended because she went home with someone
else?

"I don't," she said. "I had a terrible time."

"You didn't have to go," Scotty sounded as if he were
not to be pacified too easily. "Your folks called me up
about eleven o'clock, worried to death. How should I
know where you were? Where did you go, anyway?"

"We went —" There was a crowd gathering at the
bus stop and Sally and Scotty stopped just out of ear-
shot.

"Where?" he demanded.

"They all wanted to go to Angelo's, so I had to go

[185]

along."

Scotty looked as disgusted as her father had been.

"For Pete's sake!" he said. "That dump!"

Sally began to feel stubborn. "Well," she said, defensively, "it isn't as if I intended to go every night."

"I should think not," said Scotty. "Tell your dad you're coming home with me tonight."

The bus swung around the corner and they climbed on without any more conversation. Sally thought about Scotty's words. Had dad asked him to bring her home? She was furious at the idea.

Scotty didn't look as if he minded, but that wasn't the point. It would serve everybody right if she refused to ride with Scotty and made her dad take out the car in the middle of the night to get her.

In spite of her ill temper she made time after school to go to the hospital to see Betsy. Her little sister was spending part of the day out of bed, now. In a couple of weeks she was coming home, and the whole family were counting the days. Sally brought her a couple of tiny turtles in a flat pan, and Betsy was so delighted with them that she almost forgot her disappointment at missing the operetta.

The time she spent at the hospital always gave Sally a lift. She chatted with the three other little girls in Betsy's ward and frequently brought them small surprises too. Visiting with them reminded her of her plan to be a teacher. She still was pleased with her decision, and she would get her basic training at Northern, even if she didn't like the place too well. Thinking of the distant future, and how lucky she was not to be sick in bed like Betsy, brought the problems of today and tomorrow into a new perspective. It was pretty childish, she realized sheepishly, to make such a fuss about dad's concern for her.

"Wait till you get home," she promised Betsy. "Jean and I will sing the whole operetta for you!"

"Oh, boy!" said Betsy, her face glowing, as she turned on her radio. Her cheerful grin almost brought tears to Sally's eyes.

By the time she left for the dress rehearsal with Jean, Sally had lost most of her interest in the operetta. She dreaded seeing Eddie. Dad had extracted a promise that she would come home with Scotty, and she supposed sulkily that she might as well.

The rehearsal went as badly as everyone expected. Scotty missed one cue completely and the orchestra had to start his solo again. One of the girls forgot her lines in the middle of the first act, and another was overtaken with giggles that stopped the show for a minute. The chorus couldn't keep together and Miss Tappan looked ragged with the strain. By ten thirty she dismissed them wearily.

"All right, folks," she said, trying to be optimistic, "it was as bad as it could possibly be. That ought to mean a superlative performance according to show tradition —I hope! Go on home now, and for goodness' sake, everybody get a good night's rest for tomorrow!"

There was a confused scramble in the dressing room, as they got out of costume and into coats, with make-up still on. Jean found Sally as she was stepping out of her peasant skirt.

"I'm going to the Ranch House with Jeff," she said, looking excited. "Tell the folks we won't be late. And tell Scotty."

She tied her scarf over her head with quick jerks, looking prettier than Sally had ever seen her. Jeff grinned at her as they moved down the hall, swinging hands in time to "Dance a Cachucha." Sally felt like a forlorn old maid. Eddie and his crowd were moving toward the door together, and his eyes met Sally's without any invitation.

"Come on, Burnaby," called Scotty. "We're off!"

He grabbed her elbow and hastened her steps toward the car, where he ushered three others into the back seat and indicated that she was to ride in front. It was a short ride and everyone was too tired to make much conversation. In front of the Burnaby house, Scotty climbed out of the car and went up to the door with Sally.

"Nice seeing you again," he said, as she opened the door.

"Thanks for the ride," said Sally, too depressed to care.

"How about a soda after the performance Friday?" he asked abruptly. Sally looked up in surprise. To her astonishment, Scotty was looking into her eyes. Confused, she looked away.

"That would be fun!" she said, trying to keep her voice light. "We'll need it, I think!"

"It's a date!" said Scotty, as he took the steps in two jumps.

Sally closed the door and leaned against it, dizzy with the sudden change in her mood. Dad hadn't told him to do this! But keep hold of yourself, she reminded herself; don't expect too much, no matter what.

She woke up the next morning still tingling with excitement. Now if only she could keep it under control — not light up like a neon sign just because Scotty came around a corner.

By the end of the day she thought she had carried things off fairly well. She had *felt* like a neon sign every time she saw him in the hall, but she had managed to keep her smile gay and casual, her eyes for everyone in the group, her words as careless as if Scotty were just another boy. And she could tell that he had no idea that the extra sparkle was for him. Sally was astonished to find how easy it was: Let the remark fall that you were all excited about the operetta, and he believed you. Or that you were so thrilled about graduation being only two months away, and he thought that was the reason for your good spirits. She even took a chance on the senior ball.

"I think the senior ball will be the most glamorous thing this year," she said to a couple of girls as Scotty went past, with a sidelong glance her way. She knew he heard it, and immediately she was disturbed. What if he thought she meant she already had a date?

But she reminded herself that the ball was still a long way off. What was the use of worrying about it yet?

Thursday passed, and Friday — a long, chattery day, with almost nothing accomplished in school except talk about the operetta. And finally the big night was here.

Of course, all the Burnabys were going — mother and dad, Ricky and Jimmy. It was sickening that Betsy couldn't be there too, and they all felt it.

Sally and Jean were going early. Dad had planned to drive them out, but in the middle of supper ("It would have to be in the middle of a meal," dad grumbled; "couldn't possibly be before or after!"), Scotty called to say that he'd pick them up a few minutes before seven. When the plan was announced at the table, dad forgave the timing in his relief at being spared the extra trip.

Mother looked at Sally as if she'd been through it all herself. "Take it easy, honey," she advised. "Don't let yourself get too excited."

Did mother know she was excited about Scotty, or did she think it was the operetta? The doorbell rang sharply. The girls slipped into their coats, tied on their scarves, and waved excited farewells.

"We'll be seeing you!" called Ricky with a leer.

Sally thought of Millie. Her father had a business appointment and couldn't get there, and her mother had a very important board meeting at eight o'clock, so she wouldn't be there either. When Millie had told Sally about it Wednesday night she had looked as if she hardly cared whether she sang or not.

"Pick up your feet," said Scotty warningly. "We ought to be there by now."

They ran for the car. But even in his haste Scotty was a careful driver. He handled his car as if he were nursing it into a healthy old age. Sally felt very comfortable with him.

They were five minutes late, but their arrival went unnoticed in the flurry that was already under way. Millie complained prettily of cold hands and showed everyone how they were shaking. "Feel how cold my hands are," she clutched Sally's wrist clammily. "Joe is going to be out there. Can you imagine? I know I'll just die!"

"But you look so lovely," Sally reassured her. "Joe is going to think you're wonderful!" Millie looked grateful.

Scotty swaggered by in the colorful costume of a Venetian gondolier, well pleased with himself. A critical part of Louise's costume had been mislaid, and the whole cast hunted frantically for it. Five minutes before curtain time it turned up under a stool in the wings. The prompter was in place, rustling over the script.

Miss Tappan assembled the opening scene, and with an anxious, "Good luck, people, and keep your eyes on me!" disappeared to conduct the orchestra.

Sally felt perfectly at ease. Her peasant costume was becoming, and she knew she was going to sing better than she ever had. Perhaps it had been a mistake after all not to try for the soprano lead. Scotty's confidence had suddenly wilted, and he looked as if he were holding himself together by sheer will power.

The curtain was going up.

By the end of the first act the audience was enthusiastic. Miss Tappan came backstage for a moment to reassure them: "Just keep it up." Sally tried to peep through the curtains, but that had been sternly forbidden, and she had been sharply reproved.

The second act went off even better than the first. Sally had the sense of inspired energy that comes with success. Perhaps, after all, her vocation was the stage?

She dwelt on the idea through the next scene, following the acting with a critical eye. Consequently she missed cues, and once she stood with her mouth shut tight when the chorus burst into one of their most spirited numbers. Miss Tappan frowned at her, and Sally was ready to sink from the stage in humiliation. She was positive that everyone in the audience had marked her lapse.

After that she paid close attention to her part and *The Gondoliers* ended in a burst of rhythmic harmony. The cast took six curtain calls.

When the curtain came down to stay, and the rustle beyond it indicated the audience's departure, Sally ripped off her costume in a flurry of mixed emotions. She felt as if she had spoiled the show. But Miss Tappan

had complimented them all and said that the performance was wonderfully good. She tried not to brood
about her default, as she picked up her coat and went
out to join her family.

"See you out front," Scotty reminded her.

"That was a remarkably good show," said mother as
if she meant it.

"Good work," agreed dad, who had never liked high-
school theatricals until his daughters began to take part
in them.

"Did you really think so?" Sally demanded eagerly.
"Did you see me forget to sing once? Wasn't that
awful?"

"Did you?" mother laughed. "I must have been
looking at Scotty. He was wonderful, wasn't he?"

Sally began to feel better. If her own mother hadn't
noticed her error, maybe it was all right after all.

"Everyone did better than I ever thought they would,
from rehearsals," said Jean, appearing with Jeff. "We're
going out to eat. O.K.?"

Ricky spread his forearms coyly from his elbows,
tucked his head on one side, and capered back and forth
in the aisle, humming "Dance a cachucha, fandango,
bolero," in jig time.

"Not bad," he conceded, returning to his family. "I
might sing for them myself someday. None of those
guys had much of a voice anyway."

"Why, Scotty sounded wonderful!" Sally cried in-
dignantly. "He ought to train a voice like that!"

Scotty appeared at that minute, and she blushed.
She hadn't meant him to hear her sounding so exu-
berant about him. He acted as if he hadn't heard anything. But his glance was more than usually appreciative.

" O.K. if Sally gets a soda with me? " he asked her father.

" O.K.! " said dad, looking amused.

" We won't be late," said Scotty, striding up the aisle with Sally behind him. In the entrance hall actors and audience were milling around, exchanging congratulations. Scotty looked around for people he knew.

" Hi, Pete! Hello, Marian. There's Glen and Sylvia. And Ted. With another girl! What do you know about that? Want someone to go along with us? "

" Do you? " Sally looked straight up at Scotty, who was looking down at her. He grinned and shook his head.

" I was thinking of a twosome," he said, linking arms with her, " if you can stand it."

The Ranch House was crowded with people from the show, but they found a booth alone near the back.

" We're in luck," said Scotty, handing Sally a fountain list. She studied it carefully, twisting the curl under her ear, too absorbed to notice his glancing grin.

" I will have," she announced momentously, " a ' Special Hot Fudge ' with chopped nuts."

" The ' Sherwood Special Banana Split,' for me," said Scotty to the waitress. He sat back and looked around at the crowd. " Practically everybody in school is here tonight. I suppose the overflow is crowding the Dairy Bar."

" I'd rather be here," said Sally contentedly. He leaned forward, his elbows on the table and one hand supporting his jaw.

" Y'know, Sally, you're different."

" Am I? " Sally was genuinely surprised.

" Yeah. You've changed, or something."

She leaned forward on her own elbows, deeply interested.

"How do you mean? On account of Eddie, maybe? "

He grimaced at that, and tried to figure out what he
meant.

"No, not that. I don't know. Last fall you were so
kind of anxious. You know what I mean? " He stopped
as if he might hurt her feelings, and the waitress set
the two sundaes before them.

"I think I know," said Sally, trying to remember last
fall.

Scotty spooned up ice cream and banana and sauce.

"I kind of feel as if I could tell you now, Sally. I
thought you wanted to go steady — I just had that feeling. And I didn't. And it made me nervous."

Sally blushed at the accuracy of his diagnosis.

"I know," she said, nodding. "I felt kind of lost without Kate, I guess. Maybe I was nervous too."

He nodded. "And then there was Louise. She was
O.K. — but she got that going-steady look too. Not for
me. I didn't want to go steady, I mean."

Sally concentrated on the gooey fudge stringing from
her spoon. She didn't want to meet his eyes just then.

"I don't know why it is," said Scotty in a confessional
tone, "but there didn't seem to be anyone around that
I had as much fun with as we used to have last year.
And then you got different."

Sally laughed and looked at him directly.

"Could you say I began to grow up? " she teased.

"Could be," said Scotty, with unaccustomed serious-
ness. "Anyway, here we are again. And it feels good."

"I kind of like it too," Sally felt safe in admitting.

"That makes it unanimous," grinned Scotty. "And
how about the senior prom? "

Sally's heart began to pound heavily. This she had not expected, yet. "What do you mean, how about it?"

"What I mean is, will you go with me?"

She wanted to shout, "Will I!" She wanted, suddenly, to say, "Darling, do you mean it?" She wanted to cry out, "You're the only one I ever wanted to go with!"

But she managed to crush down the excitement in her throat, and what she said, very casually, was, "Why, Scotty, I'd love to!"

E ASTER vacation began the week after the operetta, and Betsy came joyously home. She would
have to be careful for a long time yet, but the heart
murmur had cleared up and she was out of danger.

The Burnabys celebrated her home-coming as if it
were Christmas. Mother bought her a new pair of pink-
plush bedroom slippers, with bunny-fur cuffs and sling
heels. Jean got her a deck of cards, decorated with fan-
ciful horses, and Sally contributed a tiny sewing kit and
some gay material for doll dresses. Ricky produced a
magnet, which fascinated him almost as much as it did
Betsy, and even Jimmy had done some serious shopping to find a snowfall paperweight, with a little spot-
ted dog inside. But the best present of all, for Betsy,
was the discovery that, with mother's help in the spring
and summer, she could do enough fourth-grade work
to go on to fifth with her class.

It was an eventful week, and it rushed past almost
before Sally had caught her breath. Kate was home
again, and when the crowd gathered at her house one
night Scotty called for Sally and stayed beside her all
evening. His attention was still so unexpected that Sally
could hardly believe it.

Another time he took her to a movie, and one afternoon he dropped in to see Betsy, staying until suppertime to talk to the family the way he used to do.

Spring came early this year. Overnight the grass was a thick green growth, crocuses sprang up on the lawn, the patch of scilla at the foot of the bridal wreath bushes was a brilliant blue reflection of the spring sky. Mrs. Burnaby turned to her gardening as soon as the ground was soft, uncovering tiny green spears of tulips and watching daily for last fall's new bulbs to appear.

Sally had always claimed that fall was her favorite season. But when spring came like this, fragrant with growing things and filled with daily surprises, she wanted to rush out to meet it. Fall marched into winter with a sound of drums. Spring was a lighthearted scherzo, dancing toward a gay finale.

There was still studying to be done, exams to pass, grades to make, but the crest of the effort was past. Sally could face the final weeks with carefree confidence, as far as graduation was concerned. Beyond that she refused to look. Not this spring. Not when everything else was so pleasant. If she had to go to Northern, she'd rather not think about it. There were still moments of stormy rebellion, which she locked tightly inside herself, when she felt she'd rather work in the dime store than go to Northern. But if the family didn't have any money, there was no use complaining, nor even letting them know she was unhappy. She didn't mention college plans to Scotty, and neither did he.

Scotty was coming around on Saturday nights now — almost steadily. Sally was surprised, when she thought about it, how easily they had fallen into the old groove, and how natural it seemed.

Early in April, Sally made up her mind that she would have the crowd over for her birthday on the fifteenth. When she told Scotty her plan, he approved heartily. Just their own crowd, for a sort of farewell party to their senior year. Jean could fill in for Kate — she seemed almost like one of the gang these days, anyway.

It turned out to be one of those perfect evenings. They all gathered in the recreation room, where they popped corn over the gas burner, made cocoa and, later, fudge. They danced and played cards and listened to records and talked. This was probably the last time they would all be together before graduation. During the summer some of them would be off on vacation, and next year they would be scattered. For Sally, the nicest thing about the occasion was the way Scotty hovered around her, paying attention to what she said, acting as host, as if he and she belonged together. You would almost have thought he was a little anxious himself. But Sally wasn't going to let herself count on that.

Jean was going out occasionally with Jeff these days, in a nonchalant fashion. There was a brief interval early in May when she had discovered a track star.

"I don't know how I ever missed him," she said, after he had set a new record in an important meet. "I was kind of misled with Hank and Al, I guess. Don't ever mention them to me again! The way George Brill walked into the home room! They all cheered, because of his winning the 100-yard dash, and he grinned, kind of bashful, and scooted down to his seat and looked embarrassed — he was so cute!"

"That was quite a record he hung up," said Ricky respectfully, "only I betcha he never speaks to girls."

"Yes, he does too," Jean defended her new hero. "He asked Joyce in his English class if she had done the assignment and he said he couldn't get it. She told me all about it. He has the most wonderful smile! And so much character about his mouth — sort of grim and determined. You can just tell he's going to be an Olympic champion someday."

In spite of this attachment, she seemed delighted when Jeff called for a movie or asked her to play cards with another couple at his house. By the middle of May, Jean was all through with George Brill. When Jeff asked her to go to the spring dance at St. Paul's, her pleasure was deeper than any excitement she had shown over the athletic hero.

"After all, Jeff does know how to dance," she told her family, "and he reads a book now and then. I guess maybe he and I have more in common than any of those athletes. Jeff is so comfortable! He doesn't talk about going steady, but he's always around, and it's a good thing because nobody else is."

"I think Jeff is a very nice boy," said her mother agreeably. "He has a good sense of humor. I always like to talk with him when he comes."

Jean looked pleased.

"We do seem to have a good time together. He's not really good-looking, with those glasses," she said tolerantly, "but he's easy to laugh with."

"What more do you want, for goodness' sake?" asked Sally. She had been supporting Jeff's candidacy ever since she had met him. "I think he's swell." Jean looked as if she agreed.

"Jeff is O.K.," said Ricky suddenly. "He was telling me about his dog. Now if I had a dog, I'd train him — "

Mother sighed deeply. "Sometimes I think it might almost be worth having a dog around here, just so we could stop hearing about him."

"No fooling?" Ricky sat up with a bounce. "Do you

[199]

really mean that? Why, I know where I can get the neatest little pooch — gee, he's cute, mom! And he already knows me — I found him on this newspaper route, and I see him every night, and I could buy him easy — "

Mother looked at dad. "Well," she said doubtfully, "I must say Rick's punctuality has improved. Since Easter he's only been late to the dentist's once and to dinner twice — and he's kept up his paper route longer than I ever expected. But his failing in math — "

"That time at the dentist's the teacher kept me," Ricky protested loudly. "That old Colwell didn't like me the minute she saw my face — "

"Could you blame her for that? Probably covered with dirt," Jean said *sotto voce* to Sally. Rick glared at them both.

"She didn't like me, I say, and she wouldn't have passed me if I'd had a hundred every day. She wouldn't give me a hundred anyway — "

"Now wait a minute!" Dad entered the conversation vigorously. This was one of his pet peeves. "Don't let me hear any son of mine blame a teacher for his failure. Math is math and no teacher is going to say something is wrong when it's right."

"Well" — Rick was sullen now — "I wouldn't be going to summer school if it wasn't for her — "

Dad looked very stern. "Ricky, if it takes you from now until you're ninety, you're not going to get a dog as long as you keep blaming other people for your failures. You failed because you didn't know what you were doing."

Ricky looked abused. "Well, if she can't teach math, how can you expect — "

"Now, wait a minute," dad was becoming impatient,

and Sally sighed. "You're still talking about 'her.' What can *you* do?"

Ricky gave up, spreading his hands in defeat. "I suppose I could ask you."

"You could ask. Right! That's the point. If you asked Miss Colwell, she might like you better. It's your job to find out, isn't it?"

Ricky nodded against his will.

"All right," said dad, looking more satisfied. "You go to summer school, and, if you pass your math for the session with a grade of 80 or better, you can have that neat pooch."

"Gee, honest? You mean maybe in just three months I can get him?" Ricky was beaming again. "Why, that's easy. Shucks! Why didn't you say that before? I coulda passed math before this if it had been worth-while!"

"I give up!" said dad to mother, in a hopeless tone. "Your son is beyond me!"

Sally giggled. Dad was always giving his children to mother when they were too much for him.

And then it was the last week of school. The June days were balmy, the trees were in leaf, the wind was soft. It was a lucky thing that studying was over and exams were past. No one could concentrate in such weather. Everyone was hoping for a pretty night for the senior ball.

Only five more days! Already high school was beginning to seem glamorous in memory, in spite of the problems of senior year, and Sally felt a little nostalgic when she realized that those days were behind. There was nothing to look forward to, either — just grinding along at dear old Northern, the hateful place, and living at home, where nothing ever happened.

Millie called during the last week. Sally had seen **very**

little of her since the operetta. She had appeared to be really wrapped up in Joe Ballard.

"Weren't the exams horrible?" she demanded. "I just know I didn't pass a single thing. But I should worry. I'm through with school. I've got Joe."

"O Millie, really? You mean you're engaged?"

Millie sounded shy and breathless at the other end of the line.

"Well, it's a secret, really. But I may have a surprise for you one of these days. Maybe senior ball night. Joe is taking me. But don't say anything, will you?"

Sally hung up, feeling relieved about Millie. Joe seemed to be a nice steady boy, and Millie was as much in love with him as she could be. Now she wouldn't be lonely any more.

"Five more days and we have a daughter through high school," mother said to dad, as if she couldn't quite believe it. He looked as if he couldn't either.

"What are you going to do next year, Sally?" he asked, as if it really mattered.

"Oh, I suppose I'll go to Northern," said Sally listlessly, trying not to let the bitterness show in her voice.

He nodded placidly. "I put in your enrollment last February, so that's all set. Do you still want to teach?"

"Oh, yes! But that's years away." And what dull years, in the meantime. All summer everyone would be talking about going away to college. She didn't see how she could stand it. The telephone rang and Sally jumped for it.

"Kate? When did you get in? Let's get together tonight. . . . No fooling? That's wonderful! . . . I'll be with Scotty."

She came dancing from the telephone fifteen minutes later.

"Kate's going to the prom too! Isn't that wonderful? Only five more days —"

"How about a new dress for the senior ball, for your graduation present?" Sally's depression over Northern University vanished. She still had five days before summer set in, and a new dress was always exciting. Parents did seem to know the things that mattered, more than you'd think.

Mother knew what was happening the night of the prom too.

"What are you doing afterward?" she asked, as Sally was dressing.

"I don't know exactly," said Sally, sitting before her dressing table in her slip, powdering her nose. "The idea is to stay out. Some people stay out all night and have breakfast."

Mother looked as if she were considering practical things.

"That runs into a great deal of money," she said thoughtfully. "I don't really think Scotty ought to — Why don't you go somewhere in town for sodas, and then come here to spend the rest of the time and have breakfast? You and Kate could do the cooking. I should think the boys would like it just as well — maybe better."

Sally gave her mother a quick look. "I'll talk to them," she said noncommittally. "You won't mind if we stay up all night?"

"Not with Scotty," said her mother serenely. "I wouldn't care for it with that Eddie."

Sally made a face. "With Eddie it would be simply horrible," she stated.

A car jerked to a stop outside, and she heard the door bang loosely. Scotty was waiting. Sally smiled at herself and finished her making-up with leisurely gestures. Then she slipped into her new dress. It was seafoam green brocade, with a huge skirt, a deep ruffle edging the low, round neck, and capelet sleeves. Perfectly lovely, Sally thought with dreamy happiness, as she zipped it tight. If it didn't look exactly like a size twelve, it made size fourteen seem very alluring, which was much more important. It was strange how confident she felt about this date with Scotty. She could even tell herself quite nonchalantly that if Scotty weren't around next year someone else would be.

He stood up as she came down the stairs and swished into the living room, her little gold bag dangling from her wrist. Sally knew from his expression that he thought she was lovely. And, for goodness' sake, he wasn't too sure how she felt about him! Scotty was wearing a new dinner jacket, and he had never looked so distinguished. That was odd too, because he wasn't handsome at all. The corsage he brought to her was perfect: a tiny bouquet of sweetheart roses, framed in lace, hanging from a gold cord. He took her arm possessively, as she threw her black velvet wrap about her shoulders, and they went out to the car.

"Double dates are all very well," he said almost regretfully, carefully tucking in her skirt before he shut the door, "but the way you look tonight, I'd just as soon have been a twosome."

She laughed up at him, letting him know she agreed, but that the idea was all his. It was much pleasanter to have Scotty be the one to worry a little.

The lilac bushes at the door of the high school were heavy with fragrant bloom. Scotty held her hand and lagged a few steps behind Kate and Ted, as they walked up the long walk. Small thoughtless clouds drifted across the face of the moon just over the building. The soft breeze blew a wisp of hair across Sally's face as she looked up.

"Our last night at the high school," Scotty murmured, sniffing the lilacs. Sally looked at him in surprise. She had never thought he could sound sentimental!

Then he pulled open the heavy door and held it as she went in. The gaiety from the Social Hall sounded down the empty corridors. Scotty tucked her arm inside of his.

"Did you know you're pretty glamorous tonight?" he said surprisingly. Sally smiled, entirely happy.

"If you say so!" she teased as she left him, to find the dressing room.

It was filled with girls, gay, lighthearted, bewitching, in dresses that were fluffy and full, or sleek and sophisticated, chattering about their dates as they retouched their lipstick and fussed with their hair.

Sally left her wrap and slipped out. She wanted to dance with Scotty, not to talk about him.

The music was smooth and sweet. This was no night for jive. The boys in their dinner jackets and the girls in their swirling dresses all looked older than they had the day before in the school corridors. About them was an air of being on the edge of adventure, of leaving childish things behind.

Between dances Scotty found out-of-the-way corners to sit where they would not be interrupted. He was giving her a rush, Sally realized, as if he hadn't a minute to lose and was afraid of someone's cutting in.

Millie floated by, in black marquisette, with her Joe,

looking dreamily happy. She waved, and Sally distinctly saw a small diamond on her left hand. So that was her surprise! How nice! Sally thought comfortably. She needn't have Millie on her mind any more.

Louise was there, striking in white and gold, with, of all people, Eddie Lansing! Eddie cocked an eyebrow at Sally, but he didn't speak. Scotty saw them from a distance and watched them both for a minute with an indifferent expression. "Two of a kind," he remarked, as Sally's eyes followed his. She nodded. It wasn't necessary to say more.

One thirty. In another half hour the dance would be over and graduation day almost upon them.

"Sally," said Scotty, as if he had something on his mind, "let's sit this one out. I've got things to say."

He found a couple of chairs in the balcony. In the darkness they were almost alone. One or two other couples, in the shadows, were far away.

"We can't talk when we're dancing," said Scotty sitting down facing her. He reached out and took her hands in his. "What are you going to do next year?"

Sally stifled an impulse to say something witty about creeping into a dark corner to talk about college. And then she was glad she had. Scotty was very serious.

"It looks as if I'm going to Northern," she said, with a small sigh. "The folks can't afford to send me away after Betsy's illness."

Scotty drew a deep breath. "That's perfect!" he said. "Look. I was all set to go to State. Enrolled and everything. And then mother had this heart attack, and there was a lot of fuss about my staying home. The last child she had, and all that stuff. Anyway, I'd planned to go into political science. I want to train for the State Department, you know — father's been talking that for years, and I kinda feel that way about it. So it seems that Northern University right here has one of the best political science departments in the country. Anyway, it all fits together. I'm staying home — and all I wanted to know was if you were."

Sally looked down, not daring to let her happiness show in her eyes.

"You know, Sally," he went on, "I've wanted to free-lance and not get tied down or anything. But now it's different. You're different. I don't even know how you feel about it now — but I want to tell you anyway. I'd like you to be my girl and wear my pin. That's how it is."

She was silent, still afraid of saying too much, and deep happiness washed over her. Scotty looked pleading and hopeful, as he leaned toward her. They were alone now. The other couples had slipped away to dance.

"Would you, Sally?"

"I'd love to wear your pin, Scotty," she said, feeling shy with him for the first time. His fingers fumbled with the safety catch on the black-and-gold Literary Society pin he had worn since he was a sophomore. She took it from him with a feeling of awed happiness that this could happen to her, and fastened it to the bodice of her dress. Looking down at it, she could just see it in the dimness.

"Becoming, I think!" she said, and he grinned proudly.

"No other pin would look half as good," he told her, and leaning toward her, he kissed her for the first time.

"You're my girl," he said, and it was a promise. Sally nodded. "Tomorrow we graduate — and then we've got all summer — and all next year — " his voice trailed off. Sally knew what he was thinking: all the rest of our lives. She thought so too, but she could wait now for him to say it.

He stood up and pulled her to her feet.

" Last dance! " he said, with a note of triumph. " I want Kate and Ted to see that pin! "

About the Author

Anne Emery was born Anne Eleanor McGuigan, in Fargo, North Dakota, and moved to Evanston, Illinois, when she was nine years old. Miss McGuigan attended Evanston Township High School and Northwestern University. Following her graduation from college, her father, a university professor, took the family of five children abroad for a year, where they visited his birthplace in Northern Ireland, as well as the British Isles, France, Switzerland, and Italy. Miss McGuigan spent nine months studying at the University of Grenoble in France. She taught seventh and eighth grades for four years in the Evanston Schools, and fourth and fifth grades for six more years after her marriage to John Emery. She retired from teaching to care for her husband and five children, Mary, Kate, Joan, Robert, and Martha. In addition to managing her household, Ms. Emery took part in numerous community activities. Eventually, Ms. Emery wrote short stories and books for girls becoming one of our favorite authors of the 1950s, 1960s, and 1970s.